REEL FEAR

By

Derrick Smith

Derrick Smith

REEL FEAR

By Derrick Smith

ISBN: 978-1-969800-00-9

Library of Congress copyright applied for

This is a work of fiction. Any similarity to real persons is coincidental.

Printed in the United States of America

Publisher:

Un-X Media
PO Box 1166
Independence, MO 64051
www.unxmedia.com

Dedication

For my family, Iron City Paranormal, UN-X Media, and Margie—thank for believing when it mattered most.

Chapter 1

IT'S ALL PRETEND

"So, in summation, The Bucksville House Bed and Breakfast located in Bucks County, has been found to be extremely haunted. The local stories explain that once, back around 1800, a young boy ran out into the street chasing after his ball. For whatever reason, he froze in the middle of the cobblestone road as a horse drawn carriage headed directly for him. Unable to budge, the boy was trampled under the immense power of the horse. The boy, however, was not killed by the horse. His father ran out into the street and scooped him up and carried his son into his room, where he bled to death. Minutes after the child's heart ceased beating, his father strung a thick rope above a large beam in the room directly next to his son and hung himself shortly thereafter. Max explained. He glanced over at his investigating partner. "Chuck, anything else you'd like to add?"

A little stunned, Chuck began, "Well, since then, there have been sightings here of an older man with a top hat. Sounds of a young boy's laughter have also been reported echoing throughout these halls. There has been no proof…until now."

Aaron, taping the two investigators behind his camera, took a step backward as the windows behind them slammed shut. "What the —" he murmured.

"We have footage of an image of an older man with a slight whitish glow to him walking these very halls," Chuck continued. The two investigators stood in the main hallway on the first floor of the bed and breakfast. The building was in terrible shape. The walls and ceilings were cracked and beginning to cave inward. The windows were smashed, and the floorboards devoured by termites.

Max motioned behind the pair, "Right back this way, the old man was seen pacing back and forth."

The windows once again slammed closed and then opened back up on their own. Strong gusts of wind propelled down the hall, blowing the investigators jackets and pants. The dim lights flickered violently.

Aaron stepped back even more, "Oh shit!" He backed up another two steps; he pulled the camera to his side. "Maybe we should le –" Aaron was cut off as he slammed into a thin, but muscular figure. Aaron swung around in shock, "Tom!"

"What's wrong Aaron?" Thomas asked nonchalantly.

"This is all…it's just too much," Aaron stammered.

Thomas stayed calm, "Please, just stick it out a little longer. We need you."

After some hesitance, Aaron turned back. "Okay, you're right. This is what we came for after all." He focused the camera on the investigators who didn't even notice Aaron's fear.

Tons of paper flew through the air, swirling around the camera. Another burst of cold air blew the two investigators from their stationary positions.

"Okay Max, I think we need to wrap this up," Chuck shouted over the wind. "This energy is gaining more force!"

"Go to hell!" Max bellowed. "We're staying right here!"

The house began to creak and moan. The walls shifted around the four paranormal investigators. The ceiling cracked more and more, and then it suddenly began to crumble.

"How about now?" Aaron turned toward Thomas.

Thomas shared a similar petrified look with Aaron. "Yes! Now would be a good…" He trailed off as he caught a glimpse of some movement out of the corner of his eye. Thomas raised a sole finger and motioned to a gleaming light down the corridor. "What in the…"

Aaron spun around and began to tremble and panic. "I…I…I…Let's go!"

"Max! Chuck!" Thomas screamed. The moans of the house grew louder. "Let's go! Now!"

"Not yet!" Max demanded.

The gleaming light drew closer. It appeared to take the form of an older man. He wore a tattered suit, a ripped tie, and a top hat which tilted to the side of his white hair. The walls smashed inward behind the shimmering man as he strolled toward the group.

"Look!" Aaron shouted with an outstretched arm.

Max and Chuck swirled around as they stood directly in the ghastly figure's path; it approached at an increasing rate.

Chuck swirled toward Thomas and Aaron, but noticed Max had been left behind, still immobile at the site of the elderly man. "Come on Max!" he yanked at his arm. Max wouldn't budge.

"Max!" Thomas stepped forward and reached for his other arm.

After a momentary struggle, Max plummeted backward on top of Thomas.

The building crumbled around them; the specter drew within ten feet of the group.

Chuck was stuck in Max's spot in front of the ghoul, frozen in fear. He stared directly at the shimmering man, unable to budge.

Thomas laid on the wooden floor in terror, "Chuck!" He was pulled up from behind. Max and Aaron hauled him to his feet.

"You were right Tom. Let's get out of here!" Max shouted.

"Chuck! No!" Thomas screamed back from the doorway. Too late, the figure passed through his body, seemingly turning him to stone.

"No!" Thomas bellowed as he was pulled out of the building by Max and Aaron. The three men fell through the splintering, wooden door in a heap outside of the building.

"Too late anyway," Max shouted. "This place is going to fall to the ground!"

Right on cue, a large beam crashed through the cracking ceiling straight on top of Chuck. He shattered as though he were made of glass as a thick mist of blood sprayed out from under the beam.

The bed and breakfast smashed to the earth after the peculiar events completely destroyed it as well as their close friend and irreplaceable part of their team.

- Two Years Later –

Screams echoed through the halls. Thomas ran through the dimly lit corridor as though there was no tomorrow. He screamed as loud as his lungs would allow him, "We got to get out of here!" He seemed to be speaking to anyone at all who would listen to him. Thomas was running for his life while the lights around him were flickering rapidly. He glanced over his shoulder; there seemed to be a shadowy figure approaching him. "Stay away from me!" he shouted. To no avail, the figure drew closer and closer when suddenly…everything paused.

"Very good," a voice echoed through the executive office overlooking the other colossal buildings outside. It was the voice of the executive producer of the high-powered movie and television production company, *Atomic Skyz*. His name: Alex Kinkaid.

He sat behind his large, crude wooden desk. A little over forty, gray hairs just recently emerged around the sides of his naturally dark brown hair. His thick mustache stretched around his puckered lips. He ran his thumb and pointer fingers over the unkempt facial hair. He had been overlooking the paranormal investigation show, *Into the Darkness*.

This show had been running for nearly three and a half years. It started off a little shaky, but after some guidance from Alex's company, as well as Alex himself, "Into the Darkness" shot off the charts. The team was originally run by a man named Max Angel and his partner Charles Nuzzo. Max was not as charismatic or as careful as their young assistant, Thomas Flynn. So in order to draw more of an audience, Alex made an executive decision and fired Max before the show even aired. This also took the media attention off of the devastating tragedy where Charles' life was lost and Max became the main suspect involved in their very last shoot. His involvement in this disaster placed him as the sole cause of the collapse of the house that his team was investigating during their last show. Charles' name was left out of final credits as well as all news articles relating to the incident so *Atomic Skyz* could be left out of the negative media attention and a heavy lawsuit.

At the time of the calamity, Thomas was only twenty one, barely of legal drinking age. With his thin beard and mustache and thick, black hair, Thomas was able to take the lead role with the charisma Max lacked but also kept the intelligence and knowledge Max brought to the group. Since that time, Thomas added some muscle to his five foot ten frame, upon Alex's request, in order to gain more popularity with the female audience.

This new team, Thomas always referred to it as a "crew," was composed of three members: Danielle, his new assistant, Scott, the cameraman, and Thomas, himself, acted as the lead investigator. For the first few seasons, the crew did serious investigations and experienced substantial haunting and other paranormal encounters. In the following three seasons, "Into the Darkness" crushed competitor ghost hunting shows including the likes of *Ghost Trek*, *Haunted Places*, and *Demon Watcher*.

However, in the previous three months, the show was losing viewers and its ratings had dropped rapidly. Alex's idea was to put together a gut wrenching season, full of ghosts, ghouls, goblins, serial killers, and anything else that would chill a viewer to the bone. Not exactly surprising, this type of drama is hard to find in everyday haunted houses. In order to grab the attention of new viewers, Alex hired a more 'audience relative' team of paranormal investigators for Thomas to command in each investigation.

This improved investigation team consisted of the same three members of the original, groundbreaking crew. Alex then added two others to this team, Aaron Parker and Robin Vogel. Aaron would operate the secondary camera next to Scott. Aaron actually was the original cameraman until he was released due to a lack of money. Robin was to contribute by adding the "chill" factor to the team. For Robin was a prop coordinator, she helped bring the stories to life, which the investigators told.

She seemed to make up for her deficit of camera presence with the most horrific props and fake scares ever known to reality shows. Robin was short and stood at five foot three with curly, dirty blonde hair. Her rosy red cheeks seemed to shimmer every time she walked into a room.

They had just recently finished shooting their first show as a new crew. It apparently had Alex's approval. He loved it. The show wouldn't be released to the public for another month, but the producer already had an idea of what to do with the series. He wanted to toss it in the theaters as a movie around Halloween time. This would give a big name to the show and his company; not to mention the vast amounts of money that would be earned.

"I want this to be the finale," the producer commanded. "At the end, say something like…" he trailed off. "To be continued or some shit like that," he told Thomas. Thomas looked at him a little confused. "The public loves that crap, you know?" Alex explained.

"Why do we need to do that?" Thomas asked, perplexed. "We already finished up in the warehouse."

Alex looked up from his desk. His look seemed to stare a hole straight through the investigator. "How many times do I need to tell you?"

Alex continued, seemingly annoyed, "We always need to make this garbage bigger and better."

Thomas kept quiet, even though deep down he wanted to refuse.

Alex suddenly broke the silence, "We are making a movie!"

Thomas's face went pale, "I don't know if I can do this again," he paused, "this whole…faking thing."

"Thomas, Tommy boy, you need to see the big picture," Alex attempted to convince him. "Money my man," Alex grinned. This show can bring us a fortune, if it's anything like that last one you all filmed," Alex said in a matter-of-fact tone.

"I don't know. This isn't right. We can't pretend paranormal activity is occurring," Thomas cringed.

"Well, I have no choice then," Alex stated a little perturbed. "You'll have to be replaced, just like Max." Thomas looked shocked. "You remember Max don't –"

Thomas cut him off, "Don't." He showed a mixture of anger and paranoia, "How could I not? He started this team, and you fired him. He was a great leader; I could never take his place." He paused, stopping himself from going on a rant, "You only gave me this role because you knew I needed money, and you damn well knew I couldn't abandon this show," he assured.

Alex looked a little stunned, taken back from Thomas's vocalizations. He tried to defend his decisions. "No Tom," trying to be friendly, "I hired you because you have always known what you're doing and I had faith in you from the beginning. I just…" he trailed off.

"What?" Thomas demanded.

Alex continued, "I need you Thomas. We all need you." Thomas seemed a little taken back by this. "You are the face of this show. And, after this movie, you will be the face of this company," Alex seemed very excited.

Seemingly convinced, Thomas agreed with a simple, "Okay."

Alex was pleased, "You won't regret this, but I just want to let you know, we're adding two more members." Thomas appeared a little confused. "They will be able to help your performance," Alex affirmed.

"What? Like a coach?" Thomas questioned.

"No, no, that part is perfect coming from you and your team. People like to see true fear. I am adding two actors to your lineup. I am actually meeting with them today." Alex paused, waiting for a quarrel from Thomas but it never came. "I heard they are the best in the business when it comes to reality TV, I'll send them over as soon as I speak with them."

"Fair enough," Thomas concluded. Glancing down at Alex's desk, "Why do you have everyone's profile information?"

Alex looked down at the crew's pictures scattered across his desk, each attached to a paper labeled *Background*. He answered Thomas as if he had known all along that he would ask, "Each member needs to submit a background check to the Department of Safety. In order to stay in an abandoned building for more than two days, they must approve that each person is physically well enough to lodge that amount of time without getting sick." Alex continued, "All of you will be staying in the Elizabeth Ann Asylum for as long as it takes to complete our project."

Thomas, a little startled, explained, "We have never stayed in any haunted location for more than 36 hours at a time." He paused, thinking about the money, "Although I suppose a little change is good."

Alex asked, "So we are all set? Anything else?"

Thomas responded immediately, "Two things -- When do we start? And should I get everyone to fill out those forms?"

"Yes, please, I almost forgot about those. Friday, next Friday, August 21st," Alex stated. Without any hesitation, he continued, "Meet back here in the lobby at ten in the morning and, oh here you go," he handed Thomas the paperwork. "I need these ASAP."

"A little early for a ghost hunt don't you think?" Thomas asked jokingly, grasping the papers with both hands.

Alex seemed to be rushing now. "When you get there, do you think you'll be able to jump right into it? Or would you need some time to relax?" He let out a booming laugh, "I mean it's going to take almost the whole day to transport all of your equipment and set it all up." Alex grabbed for his cell phone, "Plus I'm sure Roselyn needs time to set up her special effects bullshit."

Thomas's eyes lowered, "You mean Robin?"

"Yeah, yeah, you know, her," Alex didn't seem to pay much attention to his slip of the tongue. "Now if you'd excuse me, I have a little business to take care of. Remember," he paused, "it's all about the ratings."

Turning, Thomas mumbled under his breath, "Yea, uh thanks."

Alex just waved his arms toward the doors and gave Thomas a fake smile. "Hey, this is Alex over at *Atomic Skyz*," Alex stated speaking into his cell phone. Thomas walked out the door before he heard anything more from Alex.

As Thomas walked down the hall, he glanced over the pages he carried. Each paper asked the usual things any hiring company asked; recent employers, references, education, but there was another category. There was a full page set aside for the last grouping. It was called, *Back Story*. Thomas scoffed at this and thought, "That son a bitch is really going to put our backgrounds into the movie?"

Derrick Smith

Chapter 2

TIME TO ACT

Alex closed his door while still on the phone; he was waiting to speak with the president of the company, Darla Jackson. "Darla," he shouted excitedly, "we've got 'em."

"You better not mess this up Alexander," Darla threatened. "This can put us over the top, the best of the best, the crème' dele' crème', the –"

Alex cut her off, "I got it. I got it. I won't mess this up." He continued, "Trust me on this. It'll be our biggest and best move yet." As he awaited Darla's response, his door opened. In walked the two actors he asked for earlier in the day, one male and one female.

Darla interrupted the silence, "Like I said, don't screw this up." She hung up on him.

He looked at the receiver in disbelief before hanging it up. "How are you two today?" Alex asked, directing the question towards the male. He stood, offering his hand to the both of them.

"My name is Carrie Murtle," the woman started, shaking his hand.

"And I am Michael Reynolds," stated the other, reaching for Alex's hand.

Alex shook both of their hands then started, "Very nice to meet you both. My name is Alex." He took a breath then continued, "I am the executive producer here at *Atomic Skyz.*"

13

Carrie spoke up, "I just want to say that I really appreciate this opportunity."

"Yes, thank you very much," Michael chimed in.

"Well, I heard you two were the best of the best when it comes to this kind of work," Alex pointed out.

Michael put a smile on his face, "True. You can't get much better than us."

"Where are we going?" Carrie asked.

Alex snickered, "Ever hear of a place called Elizabeth Ann Asylum?"

The faces of the actors were drained of color, "I've heard of it, but…But isn't that place haunted?" Carrie asked. The fright appeared through her confident persona.

"I heard it's being torn down soon," Michael added.

Alex laughed loudly, "There's no such thing! And yes, as soon as we're finished shooting the movie, the building will be torn down. But that's exactly why I hired you two," he continued, "the only thing that could harm you there is the asbestos." He paused, thinking about his choice of words. He continued, "Might I add, *that* problem was taken care of years ago. There's actually nothing to worry about." He put a fake smile on his face, trying to cover his bluff.

"I think we're willing to go through anything at this point. This job means everything to the both of us," Carrie stated.

Michael finished her sentence, "Especially with the amount of money you're paying us." Carrie elbowed him.

"Don't talk about the money," Carrie whispered to her counterpart.

Alex cackled, finding humor in their bickering, "Hey, it's all about the money anyway isn't it?"

The two actors just grinned; Michael inquired, "When can we meet everyone?"

Alex also smiled, "Now that's the question I wanted to hear," he continued, "Meet them at their hotel, the Motel 6 on Robinson Street, room 116."

"Can we head over there right away?" Carrie asked curiously.

Michael added, "We would like to meet with them and try to mesh as much as possible before we get started."

"Absolutely," Alex sounded a little excited. "They should be expecting you anyway." He smirked then continued, "I'll show you the way out.

Both actors thanked him and headed for the door, "Again, thank you for this great opportunity," Carrie declared.

"Just prove your worth." Alex announced. "Oh and remember," he paused for his own dramatic effect. "It's all about the ratings."

Thomas stepped into the desolate elevator. He was on the 56th floor, so he had some time to himself on the way down. He began thinking about what he would put down for his back story; it seemed difficult to write about himself.

When he reached his dilapidated Nissan Sentra, he had his back story for the film pretty much figured out. He would begin with his education at the Philadelphia Institute for Paranormal Research then work on how he and Max met. He would then explain how they visited different locations and had only a low budget to begin the investigation show. They both had to work part time at the school's library and research center in order to fund their project. It was mostly Max's idea. Thomas could barely come up with any new ideas. He'd just elaborated on Max's unique stories and thoughts.

They ran across Aaron Parker during their second shoot. He was snapping photos of the Orleans 8 movie theater. He told them the previous week that he shot a roll of film there and saw a faint appearance in the projection booth. The two students asked Aaron if he would be interested in filming their ghost hunting show. He declined at first, but after he watched their sample introductions, where each investigator switched holding the camera, Aaron caved in and agreed to their proposal.

Even though Aaron was the only investigative team member behind the camera, he seemed to bring a special appeal to the television shows. With his buzzed, brown hair, clean shaven face, and baby blue eyes, Aaron was the only crew member who resembled a model and would appeal to females. He was muscular and rested comfortably at six foot four inches tall. When he was drafted by Max and Thomas, Aaron was in his late twenties, even though he didn't look a day over a young twenty.

That second show looked extremely professional with Aaron filming it. With his expertise, Max and Thomas knew that they could not shoot their show without him. From there on out, the three young men stuck together as a team. Aaron had connections to a top of the line production company through his girlfriend, Danielle Hartman. The small crew, as Max liked to call it, was given expensive and professional equipment and attempted to begin a television career out of their little show. This show was not all that successful so that company decided to make some "executive decisions."

Danielle brought a more active co-star role and something the group lacked, a cerebral female. At the time, she was in her late twenties and stood slightly over six foot tall. With her short brown hair, slender, curvy body, and piercing black eyes; Danielle resembled an Angelina Jolie type actress.

They fired Max based on the fact that he did not have enough spunk or charisma to be a lead investigator. Thomas was then given his current lead role.

Danielle was given Thomas's old position of assistant investigator. Aaron was also fired, and in his place they hired Scott Komen. He was a young, spunky kid who was discovered by Alex.

Scott was only in his late teens, and no one knew why he was ever hired. He was never professional, always cocky, and seemed to be more of a prima donna than anything. He constantly pulled back his thick, black hair with an open switch blade, as well as scratched his thin beard and stubble sideburns. Scott seemed to compensate for his short height with a short temper and a vulgar vocabulary.

This new team was successful for nearly three and a half years until the ratings plummeted. The company again decided to make some changes. Instead of dismissing anyone from the now tight knit team, they simply added two more members. *Atomic Skyz* once again recruited Aaron. This time, however, as the assistant cameraman. They also brought on a brand new member, Robin Vogel. She was a special effects coordinator and was to bring more excitement to the show. This seemed to be the answer they were looking for at the time. The new team only shot one show together before now going to shoot a large-scale movie. Apparently the company liked what they saw, felt the chemistry, and thought this new crew could shoot them to the top of the billboards.

After going for a ride in his Sentra, Thomas still did not understand why it was so important for the producers to have those background forms filled out. They seemed like such a waste of time. He threw them in his back seat and put them out of his mind. "I've got more important things on my mind," he assured himself.

He drove out of the parking lot and into the busy street. *Four o'clock, just beat rush hour,* Thomas thought. He sped down the street and muttered to himself, "I am so lucky this place is on the outskirts of the city." Next to the thought of losing his investigative show and the contract with Alex's company, Thomas hated traffic. That was his worst fear, he could not stand traffic, and he actually became claustrophobic when he sat in the car too long.

Thomas raced along the road, the faster he got back to the team's hotel, the faster they could get planning their stories and where they would film their important shots. Sometimes this process would take hours, maybe even days. They had nearly a week to plan and since this was a movie, they needed to have more story lines and unique effects than they ever required in the past.

Thomas finally pulled into the Motel 6's parking lot. *What a shit hole,* he thought. *Why couldn't we get a Sheraton or Hilton? Oh right, Robin didn't like us spending their money on luxury. She actually refused to stay in any ritzy hotel. She would always say, 'We're ghost hunters, not movie stars.'* He laughed at this. Thomas couldn't wait to tell them the news; he always loved proving her wrong. Now they are on their way to being movie stars and they will all be able to afford the rich hotels.

He practically ran to the crew's room to tell them about the exhilarating information from Alex. He slammed through the door, "Awesome news guys!" he proclaimed. He looked around the room, no one. He checked the bathroom, no one. He muttered to himself, "Where the hell is everyone?"

He walked outside. His car disappeared. "What the hell?" He ran his fingers through his brown hair. His near six-foot frame began to shudder. He remembered he forgot his cell phone in the car, "Shit!" he yelled. His hands shook, he was surprisingly frightened. He thought to himself, *I'm a ghost hunter but I'm scared of someone playing a childish prank on me?* He walked toward the main office, hoping he could use their office phone. A large white van pulled up behind him, the door swung open. Thomas felt a total of four hands grab hold of him and pull him inside.

Inside the van, Thomas heard chuckling. He tried to look around but only saw darkness. There was a sack of some sort over top of his head, his hands were tied behind his back, and he began to squirm. Unable to free himself, Thomas asked, "Who are you and what do you want?" There was no answer, just more laughter. It obviously provoked him. The lead investigator's patience was drawing thin. "What the fuck do you want? I have money! I have power! I can give you anything you want, just please don't do anything you'll regret!"

"Excuse me?" a female voice asked. "Something we'll regret?" She humored him, "What will we regret Mr. Flynn?"

He didn't answer, just sat panting.

"That's what I thought," said a different voice, it sounded a little raspy, still feminine though. The kidnappers laughed in unison this time.

"Wait," Thomas thought for a moment, "Robin? Is that you?"

Everyone laughed, "No shit Sherlock," said a deep voice. Aaron removed the bag from his head.

"Happy Birthday!" everyone bellowed.

"What kind of birthday present is this?" asked Thomas jokingly.

"Your twenty eighth," Danielle announced.

Aaron gently brushed Danielle's light brown hair behind her ear. He pulled her close as their lips met. "Great idea hon," he told her.

"Turn the van around," Thomas told them, "We have work to do."

"We're going' out. It's your birthday my man! No work tonight," Scott declared.

Thomas paused, then announced, "We're filming a movie you lucky sons of bitches!"

"We get to start faking again," Danielle shouted jokingly.

"That's what she said," Scott smirked.

Danielle shoved him backward, "Go to hell asshole!"

"Now we really have to celebrate!" shouted Aaron, ignoring Scott's usual rude remark.

"In two weeks," Thomas said. He elaborated, "The movie will start Friday and last another week," he paused for dramatic effect, "then we'll be millionaires."

Scott disagreed, "No," he hesitated, "billionaires!"

"Turn this heap around!" shouted Robin. "Let's make some money!"

Derrick Smith

Chapter 3

THE BEGINNING

There was a vigorous knock at the door; once, twice, three times. Thomas finally yelled out, "Would someone get that?"

Danielle stood up from her seat on one of the two beds, shuffling her maps and a mess of papers out of the way. She finally stood and hustled for the door. "I got it," she said. Danielle peered through the peephole, "Um, does anyone know who these two are?"

There was no answer, until finally Thomas spoke up, "Oh, it's probably the two actors Alex was, well did, send over I guess."

"We're getting actors?" Scott asked.

"Why do we need actors?" Danielle asked from the door.

"Just open it," screamed Thomas.

Reluctantly, she opened the door. "Hello," she offered her hand. "I'm Danielle, and you are?"

The actress reached her hand out, she was in her mid-thirties, sporting a short, red hair cut. With her other hand, the actress reached up and pushed her slender glasses back on the bridge of her nose. She seemed nearly as muscular as her companion, and spoke first, "I'm Carrie and this is Michael," she paused for a second, expecting a reaction. "We're the two actors Mr. Kinkaid hired," hoping for someone to welcome her.

Instead, she heard someone's voice from inside the room, "Mr. Kinkaid?" They all laughed. "That scumbag doesn't deserve a freaking title like mister," said Thomas from the living area. He stood up to greet the two newcomers. "I'm Thomas," he said, "I run this small group."

Carrie's partner stepped forward, his frail but tall figure towered over her. He looked to be in his late thirties, nearly as old as Alex, but Michael's hair already began to thin and his thick, Civil War era sideburns overshadowed his slender frame. "Very nice to meet you," Michael said, extending his hand. Thomas reached out to meet it. "This is Carrie," he said.

Thomas shook her hand as well. "Come on in and meet the crew," Thomas guided them into the living area. "Sorry about the mess," Thomas apologized. "We're just studying up on our maps and trying to plan out some stories and other, umm, scary shit." Thomas made quotes with his fingers. The two actors chuckled. "Danielle, you already met her; she's the other paranormal investigator."

Danielle walked back to her spot on the bed, "The official title is Assistant Paranormal Investigator," she laughed as she said it. "Anyway, we were just discussing why we need actors, can you give us any insight into Alex's plan?" she said with a little sarcasm.

Carrie shook her head, "Not a clue, all we know is that he's paying us a truck load of money."

"Yea," Michael added, "I'm pretty sure we're all yours, he never really told us of any special plans."

"Sounds good to me," Scott added, "by the way, I'm Scott." He shook both of their hands. "I'm the lead camera man. I shoot all the important storyline moments, most of the interviews, and the initial overview shot." Scott sounded very proud as he spoke those words.

Carrie added, "We can do anything from dressing up in makeup and costumes, to pretending to die, to playing the 'bad guy'."

Aaron came out of the bathroom, "Man that was a good one, whew." He looked a little embarrassed, "Oh, thanks for telling me we've got guests guys."

"No big deal," Michael said with a smile, "We're really no one special, just the extras basically."

Aaron laughed, "Good, I thought you were going to be interviewing us. Man that would have looked bad in a paper."

"I completely agree," Carrie said, snorting once from laughing so hard. Scott strolled back to the single desk in the room, checking over blueprints and mapping out shooting locations.

Thomas's tour continued to the kitchenette area. Carrie put her hand on the back of a chair, "What the…" she trailed off. She picked up her hand; it was covered in something sticky. She peered down, it was red, "Blood," she uttered.

Michael looked down, "Christ, what is that?" he shrieked, backing away. Carrie followed.

Thomas laughed, "Calm down; it's just Robin's experiments. That's what she likes to call them anyway," pointing over to the counter. The actors both seemed to regain composure, relaxing slightly.

Robin asked jokingly, "What? Don't like my toys?" She picked up a bloody arm and quickly tossed it over to Carrie. She pushed it away as the arm crashed it to the floor. "Scared?" Robin asked, laughing. "This is my specialty, scare tactics I guess you could call it," she explained.

Carrie and Michael were both speechless, "Just keep that stuff away from me, please," Carrie begged. "I hate that bloody, whorish crap."

"Careful," Thomas warned her. "This whorish, bloody stuff is our lives," he explained, "plus its good money." He put a smile on his face, "Especially after this is over."

Carrie put her head down, "I'm sorry, I didn't mean to –"

Thomas stopped her, "Fa-get abat it," he tried his Sopranos impression.

"Dude, that was terrible," Scott joked from the other room.

Danielle chimed in from the bed, "You really need to practice your impressions," giggling, "You kind of suck," she snickered.

The whole room cracked up hysterically. "What about my Ben Stiller?" he asked. Without waiting for an answer, he said, "Dew it, dew it." Everyone laughed out of control again.

"That was pathetic," Robin pointed out, nearly in tears from laughing.

"Come on, from Starsky and Hutch." he pleaded. "I thought that was pretty damn good," trying to defend himself. He turned towards the actors, "What do you think? That was pretty good, right?"

"No comment," Michael said lightheartedly, trying not to crack a smile.

Carrie put her hands up while laughing, "Hey, don't put me in the middle of this." She smiled, "I don't want to get fired."

"Alright, alright, I get it, I suck." He looked around then turned back to the two newcomers. "Get to know these guys, look over maps, whatever you want." He put his arm out and bent over, much like a butler. "Get comfortable, you've got to put up with us for about a week or so," he laughed as he stood erect again. "Back to work," he motioned toward everyone else; we don't have much time to map our plan out."

"Well," Carrie started, "at least these guys are cool."

Michael couldn't agree more as they made their way around the crew, attempting to get to know each of them individually over the next day.

Danielle was sitting on the bed, filling out paperwork, writing up scripts, and analyzing maps of the asylum. Carrie approached her, "So what's your job here?"

"Well," Danielle began, "First of all I'm filling out these bullshit papers for Alex." She elaborated, "One paper is for each of our back stories they set up for the movie and the other is a waiver." She sounded a little perturbed, "It's pretty much just so we can't sue his company if we slip and fall and break a nail or some shit."

Carrie chimed in, "That sounded pretty retarded, almost a waste." She just agreed with Danielle to be friendly.

"Yeah, I'd say so," Danielle continued, "by the way, you might want to memorize your map. These places can get pretty intricate when we dig deeper and deeper into them." She handed Carrie a copy, "Here take this."

She accepted it, grabbing it out of her hand, "Thank you, I'm sure this will come in handy." Glancing at the papers Danielle was writing, Carrie asked, "What's all that? The story lines of that place?"

"Close," Danielle answered, "it's actually the script." She continued explaining, "It's basically what Tommy and I will be reading off of during our on-camera interviews and *supposed* close encounters."

Carrie nodded her head, "I gotcha," understanding the logic. "So what's your story anyway? How did you get involved with these..."

"Goons?" Danielle finished her sentence, chuckling a little.

"Yeah," Carrie was laughing. "Do you mind if I ask?"

Danielle shook her head, "No, not at all." She thought of where to start. "Well...I haven't always wanted to hunt these ghosts. In the beginning I actually wanted to be a therapist," Carrie looked a little astounded. "Yeah, go figure," Danielle scoffed.

Giggling herself, Carrie asked, "A little ironic isn't it? Filming a big movie at an abandoned asylum -- like where you wanted to work at."

Danielle laughed again, "Yeah, really, in a sick way I guess." She continued describing her life, "I studied at Fairleigh Dickinson University over in Jersey. That's actually where I met Aaron." She paused for a moment, "Ya know he's the real reason I got into this type of work to begin with." Danielle rubbed her thumb, middle, and pointer fingers together, "I pretty much just needed money. Aaron heard the team was rebuilding, again." She let out a sigh, "I got lucky,

Alex is Aaron's uncle. He was quite reluctant to give me this shot. I mean, Aaron's not exactly on the best terms with him."

Carrie was dumbfounded, "So you pretty much got lucky to get here, huh? I guess you owe your investigating career to your boyfriend." She thought for a second, "Well, all that matters now is that you're here. You've got to make the best of this situation." Giving her a smile, "We all need this money, and this is our best opportunity." She paused, "God helps those who help themselves."

"Let's help ourselves to some sweet money then my friend," Danielle started with a somewhat anxious tone of voice.

Michael found Robin in the kitchen and sat next to her. She had papers and what looked like spreadsheets lying all around the kitchen. He fiddled with the rubber extremity she jokingly tossed to Carrie earlier.

Robin picked up her head from her work, "Scary isn't it?" Michael looked baffled. She continued, "How realistic everything is I mean."

He put down the prop, "Yeah, this actually looks real."

"Maybe it is," Robin said in a jesting tone. She winked at him, "I'm just really good at my job I guess."

"I'd say so," Michael agreed with her.

"You don't say much do you?" Robin asked him. She smiled and handed him the spreadsheet, "Alright, check this out."

Michael stared blankly at the paper, "What is it? A price list?"

Robin chuckled, "I don't care about prices when it comes to mooching off these big Hollywood companies. This is actually the placement sheet." She handed him a map with numbers and letters scribbled all over it.

Michael took the map, "Okay, now what am I looking at?" His cheeks flushed slightly, thinking that he should have known what he was looking at.

Robin pointed her finger to the number on the spreadsheet, "This is the amount of props that will be placed in a certain area." She slid her finger over to the letter, "This is the area in which that amount of props will be placed."

"Wow," he seemed impressed. "This will take hours to finish setting up won't it?" Michael questioned.

"Try a whole day," Robin corrected his presumption. "That's if we stay on task, which is why I created all these damned sheets," she finished.

Michael asked, "Where did you learn all this stuff?"

Robin stared at him, her eyes meeting his, "Well I started out attending a special effects program in Monessen. From there I bounced around a few places, getting some experience." She took a second to gather her train of thought, "I finally landed this gig on a last ditch effort. I actually heard about it through Tommy. He told me about his crew recruiting some new talent and I applied for it." She laughed to herself, "Luckily I was the only one to apply."

Michael laughed along with her, "How'd you know Tom?"

"Well it's a long story, but basically we ran into each other during one of my first jobs. He knew my boss from his first season and introduced us," Robin seemed out of breath after telling her success story.

"Well," he stated, "I'm sold on your talents and, well, your importance to this team in general."

Robin smiled, "Yeah, I know, I'm just that damn good," she finished their conversation lightheartedly.

Michael smiled and turned back to Carrie. "Ready to grab our luggage?" he asked her. He walked toward her, grabbing for the keys to his car.

"Yeah," Carrie replied. "I think I'm ready to crash for the night." They walked out to the car together, discussing their exchanges from that night. Full moon shone through the clouds, setting the perfect mood for the beginning of their long week before getting started on their biggest project ever.

The next morning Carrie and Michael ran over to the diner across the street. They were discussing what they should do with the remainder of the week. "I think we should talk to the rest of those guys and try to get to know them a little bit," Carrie suggested, taking a bite of her scrambled eggs.

Michael shook his head and swallowed a mouthful of orange juice, "Yeah, I don't see why not. After all, we do have a few more days." He took a breath and thought, "What else will we spend our time doing?"

"We can help them out if we need something to pass the time," Carrie proclaimed. "They'd probably appreciate that," she told Michael.

He finished eating his plate of French toast, "One thing at a time." Michael gulped down the last sip of the orange juice, "Let's finish hearing what the rest of them have to tell us. Remember, we are wearing these tiny cameras just like Sue asked us to do."

"Who?"

"You know, Alex's saucy little assistant."

"Oh right. Well, I guess they act as an interviewing technique," Carrie presumed. "Not something we should concern ourselves with you know," she cleaned her plate while speaking.

"Exactly, this money is all I'm concerning myself with at this point," Michael agreed with her. He took out his credit card, "I'll cover this one. Now let's get in there and finish Mr. Flynn's interviews." Without hesitation, they both headed back to the hotel room to gain more information from the investigation team.

The hotel room was buzzing, each member either on the phone or consulting one another. Carrie whispered to Michael, "I guess we can't talk to them right now." He sighed and sat down at the bar area of the kitchen.

They noticed Thomas and Danielle on the bed reviewing their lines and composing an outline of where each other would be and at what time. Across the kitchen, Robin was on the phone - apparently discussing the prop arrangements and load and unloading preparations. Scott was sitting on the armchair messing with his camera, taking it apart and putting it back together. Aaron, using a laptop on the floor, was looking up the best camera angles for asylums and circling areas on the map that would prove to be the best locations for certain shots during the filming. "Let's try to help them out," Carrie proposed.

Michael nodded his head, "I don't see why not, maybe we can finish speaking with them in the process."

"I'll head over to Aaron," Carrie told Michael. After a short moment of silence, the colleagues parted ways. Carrie headed toward Aaron, Robin's supposed companion, and Micheal strolled over to the other cameraman, Scott.

Scott sat in his armchair. He fiddled with his camera once more.

"How's it going' man?" Michael asked nonchalantly.

"Fine," Scott replied, a little distracted.

"I don't want to interrupt you," Michael pleaded.

Scott stared down at his camera, "What do you want?"

Michael's eyes grew wide, "That thing looks expensive."

"That *thing*," Scott stated, a little annoyed, "is the Silvestri Flexicam." He finally looked up, "This baby came straight from Florence and cost me 75,900 Euro."

Michael's mouth dropped, "Isn't that like 9 grand?"

Scott scoffed, "That's crazy."

"Okay, I was about to shit my pants," he joked.

"Try 95 grand," Scott stared at him, simply to see his reaction.

Michael placed his hand over his heart, "Jesus, that's…" he trailed off.

Scott turned his palms up, "Why else would we stay in a place like this?" Scott laughed, "We spend nearly all our money on upgrades, our goal is to constantly better our show."

"I'm still astounded at the price," Michael placed his hand over his heart. "I can think of a million other things to spend my money on, if I had it," he looked to the ceiling and ran his fingers through his hair.

"I can't," Scott snapped back. He stared directly at Michael, trying to intimidate him, "This is my life," he paused. "This is *our* lives."

Michael held his hands up in defense, "I didn't mean to offend you. I was just messing' around dude."

"I'm not," Scott shot back. He looked back down to his camera, "I'm the lead cameraman, and I take pride in my job, in my title." He continued to stare down, "Do not question my motives."

"I won't, I really didn't –"

Scott cut him off, "Ever!" he shouted.

"I'm sorry man, I was just trying to make friendly conversation," Michael beseeched. He turned and stood, ready to walk away.

"Why did you take this job? Do you have any idea what you two are getting yourselves into?" Scott was very stern.

Michael looked confused and sat back down, "What do you mean? This is all fake, isn't it?" He pointed toward Robin, "Why else would she be here? Why else would we be here?"

"You are all here to add to the drama or whatever you want to consider it to the movie. These places we go *are* haunted," he warned. Scott continued to explain, "Unlike some of these fakes, I *do* believe in the supernatural. I have experienced hauntings. I have captured them on film. But they never show up after production. Let me be the first to tell you though; this is all very real."

Michael was taken back, not sure what to say, "I'll be careful. I'm not here to disrupt you guys, just kind of tag along and do whatever you need."

"That's really nice, now please, leave me alone. I'm not much of a bull-shitter," Scott's head dug back into his work.

"Thank you for your insight," Michael informed him after a moment of silence. He turned toward Carrie, a little frightened now. He thought to himself, *what am I getting myself into?*

"Hey there," Aaron noticed Carrie standing beside him out of the corner of his eye. He lifted his head as he spoke.

"Hi," Carrie replied, "how's everything going?"

"Can't complain," Aaron said in a merry voice. "I really don't have anything to do," he whispered to her. "I hate cleaning my equipment and I have my maps all planned out already," he explained.

Carrie looked surprised, "Wow, you're quick. Everyone else is still busy as hell," she continued, "I mean look at Scott over there, he looks pretty intense."

"He is." Aaron smiled, "You might want to tell your friend not to bug him while he's doing' his stuff." Aaron picked up a map, he faked memorizing it. "I guess I would too if I spent 100 grand on a freaking camera," he laughed. "Don't ask. I don't know why he did."

"I guess you're a mind reader too," she chuckled under her breath. "I can see what Danielle sees in you," Carrie smiled.

"Please," Aaron said jokingly, "tell me, cause I don't."

"Charisma, humor, good looks –"

He cut her off, "I was kidding. I really don't want to know."

Carrie smiled, "I figured." She let out a sigh, "So what's your story? How's such a nice guy like you get involved in this tasteless line of work?"

"First off," Aaron warned, "I wouldn't talk like that around these guys. They get pretty serious about this type of work."

"Oh, sorry," Carrie told him.

He shook his head, "Don't worry about it, I know this is a job. I don't really believe in ghosts anyway. This is just good money." Aaron looked around the room, "Just be careful who you say that kind of stuff to, is all. Anyway," he paused, "I went to school in Philly for photography. I was actually begged to join their original team, you know, before they broke it up twice."

Carrie nodded her head, "Yeah, I think Michael and I have heard about that before." She paused, "That sounds like they fucked you over that first time around."

Aaron laughed, "Or you could think of it the way I think about it," he snickered, "they just gave me a break." He gathered his thoughts, "Before they broke us up, and even before we received our TV contract, the three of us traveled all over the nation."

She interrupted, "Really? That I didn't know. I just thought you did more local jobs."

"We did, for a while..." he broke off.

"What happened?" inquired Carrie.

Aaron looked past her, "Well, we weren't making any money, and we started arguing. Both Thomas and I agreed Max was making bad decisions and well..."

Carrie could tell that this was a sore subject for him, "You don't have to –"

Aaron stopped her, "It's fine; I just haven't talked about it for a long time." He took a breath, "Anyhow, long story short we tried to come up with ways to get rid of him." He sighed, "We realized our best way to get rid of him was when we signed our big television contract. We asked my Uncle Alex if he could help us. At that time he wasn't a producer, just some hiring specialist." He stopped, "See, I'm not sure of how much of this you're supposed to know, so just don't say anything."

Carrie nodded her head, "Of course, of course. Not a word, I promise."

"To get around legal crap, like conflict of interest and shit, they pretended to fire me. Well, that's why I say it was time off, because it was more like a sabbatical," Aaron explained. Carrie understood and remained silent, believing his story had almost concluded. He continued, "I wanted back in it, I wanted to make a name for myself. The money was good from that job, but I was still a nobody. I wanted, well still want, more."

Carrie attempted to finish his sentence, "So that's why you wanted a part of this movie. It's sort of a way to get back to where you started and finish it."

"You got it babe. You hit the head on the nail, or um, nail on the head," Aaron laughed at himself, Carrie chuckled alongside him.

She put her hand on his, "Thank you for sharing. That must have been difficult."

"Eh, a little bit. It was more the actual remembering part that was difficult," he pointed out. Aaron pointed to Scott and Michael, "Sorry to interrupt you but you might want to go rescue your friend," he gave Carrie a soft smile.

Carrie noticed Michael looking around, most likely looking for her to give him a hand out of the awkward situation. "Thank you," she told Aaron. She stood up to give Michael a hand.

"Not a problem," Aaron said, "just please don't tell anyone what I told you."

"You have my word," Carrie promised him, knowingly lying. She headed over to save Michael from any further humiliation.

The crew headed to bed early that night. Thomas had announced that the team would move out early the next morning to pick up their equipment in order to test it before putting it to use. Michael and Carrie stood outside of the room, discussing their plans for the upcoming week.

"We got our interviews," whispered Carrie, she tried not to wake anyone.

Michael lit his cigarette, "That's half the battle, next objective: plant the pinhole cameras."

Carrie turned away from the smoke and questioned, "These guys are professionals. Why do we need to put these things on them?"

They both pondered to themselves. Michael puffed his cigarette, "I don't really know. Maybe the production team needs different types of footage that Thomas refused to."

"Who knows? Those company bigwigs are so secretive. I can't trust them. I know that much," Carrie declared. "I just want my money for being with these weirdos," she laughed.

Michael laughed along with her. He inhaled on the butt of his cigarette, "Damn straight, they're accepting us so easily. This is going to be a cake walk. They don't even want us here."

"Well, we better get back in and get some rest," Carrie suggested as she turned toward the door. "Finish your death stick and get in here…six a.m.," she mumbled under her breath and gave out a loud moan.

"I'll be in, let me enjoy this. Alex's papers said no smoking in that place, and it sounds like these fuck ups want to get started early," Michael muttered tiredly. She waited at the door as he requested. "Alright, I'm coming," he finally said.

"Now, let's hurry and put those camera things on all their stuff. I'm tired," Carrie said as she opened the door very slowly. She held her pointer finger up to her mouth, "Quiet."

Carrie turned over in her sleeping bag, "Where'd they go?" she asked Michael.

He rubbed his eyes, "What? We aren't leaving till –" He looked at the clock. "Shit, fifteen minutes ago," he yelled out. He jumped up, right out of the sleeping bag.

"We can't go without them," Carrie proclaimed. "We're following them there. There's no way we can make it there on our own," she began to panic.

"Calm down," Michael attempted to compose her. He looked around to see if they had left any directions. Nothing was left. "We don't even have our maps they gave to us," Michael observed. He ran out the door in hopes that they were outside.

"Where are you going?" Carrie shouted toward him. She tossed her glasses on and pulled her pants and hoodie on as fast as she could. "We need to pack our stuff!" She followed him out the door.

There they were, packing up the van. "Something wrong?" Thomas yelled, he noticed the two actors running out the door.

The two newcomers stared off in disbelief. Smiles grew upon their faces. "No, not at all, we were just, uh…" Carrie stammered.

"We thought you left," Michael laughed. He nudged Carrie, "Sorry we're late."

"No worries," Thomas replied in a friendly tone. "Just get your asses down here to help us pack up," he joked with them.

The two actors turned back to the room. "You got it. We'll be there in a sec," Carrie assured the rest of the team. They hurried into the room and scurried right back out, all in less than a minute.

"Good to go," Michael announced as he stepped outside the rundown hotel room. He and Carrie rushed their luggage to their car. "What can we help you with?" Michael asked a little sarcastically.

Robin pointed to a large, brown, cardboard box. "Can you toss that in your trunk?"

"Sure," he said graciously. He bent over to lift it. "What the hell do you have in this thing?" Michael asked as he struggled with its weight.

"A little of this, a little of that," she answered, joking with him.

"What, not man enough?" asked Scott. He did not laugh.

Michael knew he was not joking but laughed anyway, as he tried to keep from creating any tension. He lifted the box with a grunt. "Seriously though," he paused, out of breath, "what do you guys got in here?"

Thomas explained, "It's just all those damn papers we had to fill out. There are some maps in there; I believe a camera, and a few small E.M.F. meters." He acted somewhat shy, almost as if he were hiding something.

"E.M.F. meter? Electro…magnetic field meter?" Carrie took a stab at the abbreviation after hearing about them on television.

"That's right," Thomas clarified. "It helps us pick up paranormal activity…"

"I get it," Michael started after being ignored. "This is one of those don't ask don't tell situations, right?"

"You think he's lying?" Scott was angry.

Carrie jumped between the two men. "Okay boys, a box really isn't that important," she tried to point out.

They finally backed down. Michael slammed the trunk closed. "You're right," he agreed with her. "When are we taking off anyway?" he asked as he tried to change the subject.

Danielle walked up to him, "Does now sound good to you two?"

"Fine with us," Carrie stated.

"Let us grab our stuff from our room," Michael nearly shouted. "Then I think we're good to go."

The two actors headed for their room. In a little over five minutes, they exited with a few bags in each hand. Carrie apparently ditched her glasses for a pair of contacts, "Let's get this show on the road."

The paranormal crew filed into the bulky, white van and the two actors got into their shiny black BMW. The van paved the way as the two actors followed. They were headed to Alex's office to pick up their supplies.

The two vehicles pull up to the *Atomic Skyz* office building. Upon arrival, they spotted a large 18-wheeled truck. "Whoa," Aaron said, "what's that for?"

"Take a guess," Thomas replied, passing him a smile.

Robin chimed in, "We do have a lot of props to transport, as well as, set up when we arrive."

They pulled up and rolled the window down as they spotted Alex waiting outside to greet them. "Welcome back, everyone," he announced. "This will be our first step to fame." He moved away from in front of the truck in an attempt to reveal it to the crew. "Let's start loading up," Alex said, sounding excited.

Everyone from the crew exited their vehicles after parking on the side of the building. Wearing their over coats, they circled around their leader. "Alright guys, time to get to work," Thomas commanded. Everyone headed toward the building. They acted as if this was routine, which truthfully, it was for the small band of bottom of the line, paranormal investigators, who were certainly soon to be rich.

"What do you want *us* to do?" Carrie asked curiously. Michael peered out the window of the car, retaining the heat by hunching down inside. "Stay warm," Thomas shot her a smile; she turned back toward the car with Alex at her side.

"You got it, right?" Alex whispered in her ear once he realized Thomas was finally out of ear shot.

Carrie nodded her head, "We have the backgrounds and planted the spy cameras. Some interesting stuff, you know?"

"Of course. I was involved in most of it," Alex snickered. "Whatever you heard, forget it," Alex explained. "You'll get your money, just don't ask any questions." They arrived at the car. "Tell your buddy what I just explained to you. I've got to head back to the truck." He spun around, "I just don't trust those ungrateful bastards."

They all shared a smile. Carrie and Michael settled into their luxurious BMW. "Enjoy this now," Carrie explained. "When we get to that building we won't have any heat or luxury. Hell, we'll be lucky to have a seat at all." Both actors cackled, laid their seats back, and rested their eyes.

Thomas caught up with the others walking toward the building. After about fifteen minutes, the crew strode out of the building, one by one in the direction of the large, 18-wheeled truck. Each member carried some crate, gadget, or mechanical article. They placed each individual piece inside the back of the truck. After nearly two hours of loading, the truck was full of horrific entities and mechanically controlled units. "Let's grab some food," Danielle declared, as she wiped the sweat dripping from her forehead.

The crew followed her and Alex in the direction of the cafeteria inside the building, which was located on the ground floor. "So, we're ready to head out?" Alex asked.

"I'm pretty sure we are," Danielle responded. "Just as soon as Robin finishes her inventory, we can go."

"That's great news!" Alex proclaimed. "The sooner the better really; we are on a tight schedule." Alex continued, "The longer we stay in that abandoned building, the more money it will cost this company."

Thomas caught up with the two in the lead, "I'm pretty sure we can finish this in a week," he confirmed. "So there's really no reason to worry boss," he said in a sarcastic tone.

"Good, cause the more money we spend, the less everyone gets," Alex explained. "Now let's get some chow before we head out on our long journey to 'hell,' so to speak," he joked.

The two investigators looked at each other in confusion. "Wait, wait," Danielle stopped Alex. "You're coming too?"

"Of course," Alex responded without hesitation, "I'd like to see the place where we will make our fortunes." He paused, "Plus, I really don't trust you with my truck," Alex laughed along with the team.

They all made themselves comfortable in the lavish cafeteria. Because the crew would be locked inside an abandoned building for at least a week, maybe more, they devoured excessive amounts of food, on Alex's bill nonetheless, and then headed back outside. "Let's get moving," Alex said. "There's only about three hours left of daylight and I'd like to head back with my truck by then," Alex stated, confidence shown through his voice, money on his mind. The investigation team loaded into the van, the actors started their BMW, and Alex mounted his truck, alongside his driver.

Chapter 4

THE ROAD AHEAD

The asylum was a good half day drive away from the office building. The trip took them through three states, down highways, and finally twisted them around dirt roads. The 18-wheeler had some trouble navigating down those derelict roads, so it took a little longer for Alex to arrive; nearly an hour longer than the rest of the members.

As the 18-wheeled truck pulled up to the front gate, the tall, brick asylum loomed overhead. It was situated nearly a half mile behind the gate but still blocked out the sun, positioned in the sky behind it. The red bricks of the structure were rotted and began diminishing years ago, Alex thought. Thick, grayish vines climbed the sides of the asylum's brick laden walls.

The road they traveled looked as though it were originally made of cobblestones, but now they were chipped away leaving few stones intact. The truck bounced over the holes, nearly tipping over. Alex noticed that most of the windows were still in one piece. Old steel bars surrounded them, most likely to keep escaping inmates, or employees. The doors were just recently replaced by *Atomic Skyz*, as well as the west wing. This was all for the investigators' comfort. They also installed lights powered by a generator which was purchased and installed by *Atomic Skyz* and their contractors.

As they drew closer Alex noticed the vines appeared to reach out toward the new visitors' vehicles, parked near a large apple tree, apparently dead, but somehow still producing fresh apples. Alex looked up into the windows; he noticed a figure seemed to move behind it. He let out a slight gasp and asked his driver with curiosity, "Did you see that?"

"You'll see a lot of things at this place," the driver replied, "I was here once and saw enough for a lifetime."

"No way this place is only thirty years uninhabited," Alex muttered under his breath. He apparently tried to hide his fear.

"I heard this place went downhill even before it closed," the truck driver explained. "No one ever cared about that place – or the people in it."

Alex didn't flinch. "Well," he began, "it should make for a good backstory." Alex let out a chuckle.

His driver looked over toward him, "I wouldn't laugh if I were you. This place has taken many lives in the past." The building loomed overhead, it was only one story tall, but had pillars and towers which reached toward the sky. It was mainly constructed from red brick and mortar, but some spots seemed to have been replaced over the years with concrete slabs and multiple colored bricks. Vines were overgrown and covered most of the building, wrapping around the gates beyond the windows to keep the inmates sealed inside. The windows were tall. They stretched from halfway up the wall all the way up to the roof joists coming to a point directly below the roof. They pulled up beside the building, in a position ready to unload. "I'm sure it's ready to take quite a few others," the driver warned.

"Let's not waste any time," Alex told the driver as he jumped out of the seat. "Back this heap up and I'll get the crew to unload her."

"You got it boss." The driver pulled forward then began backing the truck up into position, directly in front of the old fashioned, metal, barred, double doors.

Alex pushed the doors; he needed all his might just to swing them open. "Come on guys, let's unload and get this million-dollar project in progress," his voice echoed down the hallways.

The crew was placed in the convalescent wing of the building. The wings were separated between those who may one day be released and the life patients. These two types of patients were split with a high security hallway, right in the middle of the building; there was nothing but gypsum board and shattered counter tops that remained. Three dining rooms sat at the ends of each wing, separated for the employees discretion of the residents; those who acted up during the day would not be given dining room privileges.

The life patients were then split amid a violent division and a general patient division. Right beside the violent wing laid the church which was still pretty much intact after all those years. Next to the church was the laboratory, treatment room, and directly outside -- the cemetery. In order to reach the morgue however, the doctors and patients entered through the small precautionary center then through the secure room. Only through the security room could the laboratory be accessed, mainly so the old occupants never knew what actually took place behind the condemned walls.

Across the hall from the chapel, the seclusion room was placed, used most of the time to house the mentally unstable next in line for the mad doctors' experiments and *treatments*. This room was seemingly in the best condition, according to the construction map. Directly next to the seclusion room sat the entrance to the basement, which was mainly used to house the boiler systems. The door was just recently replaced and locked according to the map; the contractors who evaluated the building obviously did not want anyone exploring that area.

The map was supposedly updated recently, however, there were multiple areas on the map that seemed to be missing or faded out. The area around the laboratory and the area behind the church appeared to be blackened or distorted the most.

Thomas tossed his suitcase on his queen sized bed. "Wow, this place is amazing!"

"Amazingly dreadful," Danielle walked in right behind him. "They shouldn't have updated this wing. It's just not right."

Scott brushed past her, "Who cares?" he asked in disgust. "At least they made the old place habitable for a short time. I wouldn't have stayed here if they didn't." Scott tossed his suitcase down, then, very gently, set his camera on his bed. He treated it more like a child than a piece of equipment.

"Four beds in one room…" Thomas pointed out, only to get cut off.

"Great observation Mr. Investigator," Scott mocked him.

Danielle stared at him, annoyed, "Do you always have to be such an ass?"

Scott just smiled. A voice from behind him shouted, "Whoa, harsh words Lil' missy," attempting to impersonate John Wayne. Aaron poked his head through the doorway. "So what are we doing about sleeping arrangements?"

Thomas scoffed, "Sleep? There's no time for sleep. They wasted their money on this wing."

Robin was the last crew member to walk in. "We'll have to split up sleep time," she suggested. "Regardless, we all need to explore this place," she smirked. "After you let me set up everything to scare the living crap out of you," she appeared quite anxious.

"Where are the two actors?" Aaron asked, "Are they lost already?" He shared a laugh with everyone.

"No, we're right here," Carrie stated as she stood in the doorway. "This place is exhilarating," she took a deep breath and looked back toward Michael who walked in right behind her.

"It's as if the old psychiatric crew just packed up and left," Michael pointed out. He pointed toward the broken-down security room, on the other side of the hall. "I mean look, there are random wheelchairs and gurneys just sitting there, old bandages waiting to be put on some crazy. There's no way this was a planned evacuation."

"Evacuation?" Thomas laughed, "There was no evacuation here."

Carrie and Michael looked puzzled. "Then why is all this," she stammered, "stuff lying around?"

Danielle looked to Thomas as if waiting for approval to answer the question. After a moment she addressed the entire group. "There were

Derrick Smith

plenty of incidents dealing with patients and doctors, but…" She trailed off.

Thomas picked up after her, "What she was trying to say is that the last event that took place here was the worst and, well, the bloodiest in any type of hospital, ever. There was…," he thought, "a massacre of sorts."

Carrie's mouth gaped open, "You mean a patient versus doctor sort of thing?"

"Let me guess," Scott presumed. "The patients tried to escape, and the doctors tried to stop them. One thing led to another, and the patients overthrew the doctors, giving them the treatments the patients adorned?" After finally taking a breath, Scott looked at Thomas very confidently. "Am I good or what?" he smirked.

Thomas glanced up, before he was able to speak, Danielle stepped in, "No, you're actually not!" Her face flushed, "It's actually quite the opposite. The doctors just killed their patients, supposedly performing new 'treatments' on nearly every single one."

Before Danielle was able to go off on a rant, Thomas cut her off. "It's okay. I'll take it from here." He placed his hand on her shoulder, and she grasped it tightly.

"I'm sorry guys, it's just," she swallowed hard, "My grandfather was one of the patients here, and there is no record of his history." Danielle continued, "Or body for that matter, after the massacre."

Aaron hugged her, "It's okay baby, I'm here." She looked up and gave him a soft smile.

Thomas looked over to Danielle, "Do you mind if I continue?" Danielle just nodded her head. She remained silent. "Well to take you back a little," he took a deep breath before he continued, "The doctors at this place were, how should I say this? They were not afraid to experiment." As Thomas glanced around the room, he noticed everyone had taken a seat and looked up to him in awe. He carried on. "They lost patients here quite frequently. The doctors did everything from new versions of frontal lobotomies, to experimenting with drugs, to reverting back to the medieval time, removing organs and body parts, thinking they were the cause of some sicknesses. Now these doctors weren't the craziest at that time, but they never really showed any concern for their patients."

"What do you mean craziest?" Robin asked him, suddenly curious.

Danielle jumped in to answer for Thomas, "Doctors back then didn't have a lot of training when it came to mental illness."

Aaron cut in for her. "I studied this stuff and they experimented on patients in some places, but..." he trailed off and scratched his head. "I didn't think they did that in this area or even during this time period."

"You're absolutely right, it started here," Danielle stated. Everyone in the room stared off expressionless in her direction. "Those experiments or so called *explorations* began here," she continued as she began to tear up.

Aaron wrapped his arms around her as tight as he could. "It'll be okay. I promise." He tried to comfort her, but it was too late. She began sobbing into his shirt.

Thomas placed a stern hand on her shoulder, "I'm sorry, Danielle." He pulled his hand away as she turned toward him.

"Thank you," she sobbed, "please finish the story for me."

Thomas nodded his head then continued the tale, "The ultimate downfall of this horrific hospital was the experiments. You see, the doctors began attempting new procedures and ways to cure patients. They needed money for these to continue. However, their hospital was not producing successful recoveries and their experiments were not leading to cured mental *oddities* as they sometimes put it." He took another breath; thinking he may have gone overboard with his story, until he looked at everyone. Their eyes agape, mouths drooping, apparently very enthused, even Danielle. He looked down before he commenced once again, "Their loans were not being paid back, and the hospital was going to be foreclosed. The doctors went power hungry. They grew just as insane as the patients."

Carrie jumped in, "So the doctors knew they wouldn't have much longer to do their experiments. How long before it closed?"

"I'm not exactly sure, but maybe four to five days," Danielle explained.

"And that's why the body count was so high," Thomas' voice softened. "The doctors tried to perform as many experiments as possible. I don't believe they even record them."   Michael seemed disturbed, "I can't believe that. It's cruel. It's inhumane. It's —"

Robin cut in, "Evil, merciless, heartless, brutal, appalling, take your pick." She seemed to be offended but at the same time interested.

"Calm down now," Aaron begged her, "He's just trying to explain the occurrences of this putrid building's history."

Danielle puckered her lips and smiled. She obviously knew he was correct.

"May I?" Thomas asked with a very comforting voice. No one disagreed with his request. Therefore, he continued the brief history lesson. "They simply dumped their bodies in the basement, and made other patients work night and day to burn their fellow comrades."

Danielle jumped in again, "Basically, there was no progress ever made and the hospital foreclosed. The doctors were taken into custody for cruel and unusual punishment. They were later released, no charges against them. The patients apparently did not try to escape or evade 'treatment' in any way, but they were punished for something they did not do," Danielle slowed down; she realized she blurted her story out unexpectedly.

"No patients were ever found though," Thomas helped her out. "There were plenty of stories, but eyewitness accounts repeatedly saw the doctors, dressed in green jumpers enter the building on their own free will."

"What were they doing there?" Scott asked.

"Probably finishing their experiments," Robin guessed.

Danielle spoke up again, tears creeping in her eyes, "They burnt them, all of them."

"That was never proven," Thomas took a breath, afraid he would offend Danielle, "But there was evidence to support the idea."

Danielle seemed to calm down slightly. "Right, the cops eventually searched the blast furnaces and found nearly twenty-five more patients' charred bones, after they had already emptied it once."

"But there's no proof," Scott scoffed, nearly laughing in their faces. "I don't believe a word of it."

"Believe it or not," Thomas paused, "it most definitely happened."

There was a loud moan reverberating through the halls, "It's time!" That's all the voice said, "It's time!" The group shuddered. They huddled around Thomas, all except Scott.

"Are you all serious?" Scott asked. "What do you think that is? A ghost?" he laughed hard. Holding his hands out in front of him and walking toward the group with a limp, "Ooo," he messed with them. "I'm the ghost of a crazy doctor! I'm here to claim your souls. Ooo," Scott joked.

Danielle hit him hard, "Stop! That's not funny!" She grabbed Aaron's arm and pulled him out of the room. They both gave Scott a perturbed look as they exited the room; they headed toward the echoing sound.

"Asshole," Aaron muttered under his breath. Scott smirked and turned away.

Thomas took control, "Come on guys, we are still a paranormal investigation team." He waited for someone, anyone to speak up and join him. "Anyone?" he asked. Scott grabbed his camera as Carrie stepped forward.

"I'll give it a go," Carrie announced. "I'm here. I might as well make the best of it." Thomas smiled at her proclamation.

Scott stood in front of both of them, "You need a camera man don't you?" Again, Thomas smiled.

"Thanks guys, let's go," Thomas directed them out the door. He looked back to the two left behind, "You're sure you're not coming?"

Michael lifted his shoulders, slightly embarrassed, "That's not exactly my thing."

Carrie shot him a dirty look, "Why'd you take this gig then?" He just looked down, as he sat down on one of the beds.

"I'm going to unpack and start looking around to make sure the maps are right so I can set up our props when they come," Robin explained.

"Okay then. Let's catch up with Danielle and Aaron." Thomas stated. Anxious to explore, he turned away and headed out the door.

The group finally grew close enough to the voice that they could see its origin. It was being produced by a tall, dark figure. Granted, everything was gloomy in that hell house. "It's time, let's go," the voice declared. "We're a little late, but we got stuck on the dirt roads."

"Alex?" Danielle asked, "Is that you?"

"Of course. What? You thought it was what? A ghost?" he laughed, much like Scott had. "You guys are so predictable."

Thomas chuckled to himself. He thought he was crazy to believe they would actually experience a poltergeist. "A little late?" he said jokingly. "Try an hour and a half."

Danielle and Aaron stood expressionless. They stared at each other for a moment. They suddenly burst out in laughter.

"I can't believe we thought he was a ghost," Aaron blurted out, as he ran out of breath.

"You guys really did? Wow, I thought I hired professionals." Alex nudged Thomas, apparently joking. "Why are you all so jumpy?"

Carrie explained to him, "They just finished telling us the story of this building's abandonment."

"Oh God, you're already trying to scare our newcomers?" Alex asked, somewhat surprised. "You've done this before, but I think it's a little unnecessary in this place and time," he stated.

"I'm not trying to scare anyone," Thomas defended himself.

Danielle backed him up, "He's right, I know the building's history," she paused as she tried not to get choked up again. "He didn't lie. This place really *is* that messed up." She drew close to Aaron; she felt his body next to hers and immediately felt calm.

Alex jeered off once more, as he pushed the issue aside, "Well whatever, I won't mess with your *investigation*. I just want to get this underway and get the truck back." He glanced up at the crew, "Time is money, you know?"

"Alright, let's go get Robin and Michael to help us out," Thomas suggested. "She needs to tell us where to put everything anyway," he explained.

Alex turned back to the hall where he came from. "I'll get the driver to prepare the truck to unload. Just hurry up if you don't mind."

"You got it. What do you always say?" Thomas asked sarcastically, "It's all about the ratings, right?"

Carrie scratched her head, "Does that really apply here?"

"No, but the faster we unload, the faster we film. The faster we film, the faster we put the movie into theaters –" Thomas was cut off.

"And the faster we get the ratings," Alex announced as he finished his sentence. Alex walked his own way, and the crew walked theirs'.

Danielle looked up to Aaron, "I just want to get this done."

"Same here, something just doesn't feel right," Aaron agreed with her.

Thomas chimed in, "I know what you mean. I get the same feeling." The three crew members and single actress stepped back into their double-bedded chamber.

The crew sauntered to the truck, one by one. Their faces all showed eagerness to begin their motion picture project. Alex waited at the entrance of the asylum, "Come on everyone! We've got some work to do."

Outside the battered walls of the asylum, the 18-wheeler waited. It was backed up to the entrance way, the trailer's mouth wide open. Inside the massive vehicle sat millions of dollars in high powered, fright enhancing devices -- all paid for by *Atomic Skyz*. "I can't wait to start setting this stuff up," announced Robin. "This is so exciting, I've never worked with so much expensive equipment before," she smirked. "This is going to be thrilling."

"I'm glad you're so thrilled," Alex applauded her. "Now can we start unpacking?"

"Yes sir." Thomas saluted him, "Right away sir!" He moved his hand around his mustache as if to admire his audience.

The group cracked up at his sarcasm.

Alex flipped off all of them with both hands. He laughed and walked into the darkness of the trailer. Suddenly, a glow lit up the trailer. Alex had turned on the trailer light. Its dim radiance was just enough to shine on nearly every square inch of load it carried. The light reflected off the grotesque figure props packed into the back of the haul. There were also crates upon crates overflowing with fake blood, mechanically sound apparatus that was created specifically for this production. Its purpose was to operate the horror figures and all other devices to scare the crew as they made their way through the building. "So where do you want all this, Robin?" Alex asked before he allowed everyone to enter the truck.

"Um, how 'bout we just put it all in our hall in the new wing for now? While everyone does their introductions and solo interviews, I can sift through it and get it all sorted out," Robin suggested. She was the first one to jump up into the back of the 18-wheeler. "All of the heavy paraphernalia is toward the back, so would all the men come back here and get started?" she asked very politely. "Everything up front is lighter; the ladies should be able take most of that in."

Thomas stepped forward, "Alright guys, you heard her. Let's get to it."

The four men climbed aboard first; they headed as far back as they could go. "Should we go two by two for each crate?" asked Aaron.

"You need help with one of these?" Scott scorned. He picked one up, nearly toppled over before he gained his composure. He made his way past the object in the haul with little difficulty. The three others laughed as he made his way to the entrance of the asylum. He eventually made his way into the building, disappearing into the vast shadows that began to overrun the structure.

"Now that he's out of the way…" Thomas trailed off. He shared a laugh with the others. "Two people per crate. The extra can grab some of those figures and props," Thomas pointed to the side of the trailer while he took the lead.

As Michael reached down with his gangly arms to measure the weight of the first crate, he groaned. "Oh God, this is heavy. What's she got in here?" he motioned with an outstretched finger as he glanced up to Thomas.

"Remember don't ask, don't tell?" Aaron asked. He looked over to Thomas. Aaron noticed a quaint smile grew on Thomas's face.

"Gotcha," Michael answered. "Let's get this thing inside." He and Aaron picked up the large, wooden box. They moved very slowly out of the truck. They groaned every step of the short trip.

Thomas looked around. He realized he was the only one left in the trailer, and he noticed Alex was engaged in a conversation with the women. They stood directly outside of the haul. The trailer seemed extremely gloomy and ominous at a first glimpse. He picked up a plastic body, some sort of mechanical contraption shaped like a car lift, and a large bag filled with medical knives and scalpels. He looked back to see the women reaching for tiny boxes and lighter objects toward the opening of the trailer. *These objects were more of a female caliber anyway*, he thought. He followed the others inside. He knew they had much more work to do.

It took nearly two hours to empty the rear of the 18-wheeler. Every member was exhausted after they lugged all of their equipment and props out of the truck into their wing of the asylum. They all sat, strewn about their room.

"Feels like dinner time," Scott exclaimed from his place on one of the beds.

"You cooking?" Danielle asked. Her patience grew thin from Scott's rude comments.

Scott shot up in surprise, "You're the woman," he let out with a rude chuckle.

"You're a jerk," Robin yelled from the ground. She sat beside Scott's bed. Danielle and Aaron lay on the opposite side.

Thomas stood from the bed he and Robin were sitting on, "Come on guys. We haven't even been here five hours and you're already arguing." He gave Scott a dirty look, "Come on, grow up."

Robin stood up and headed toward the door, "I'll get started sorting our stuff." She looked out into the hall. It was cluttered with everything from the trailer. From floor to ceiling, wall to wall, their props filled the hallways. There was barely a path to get through. Alex shuffled through the mess as Robin walked out into the mess.

"Wow, how much money do you think we've got here," Alex joked with her. He finally reached the room after he excavated his way through it all.

"A lot more than any of us are worth," Robin mocked him.

Alex smiled, "You aren't kidding."

Robin strolled down the hall toward the entrance of the asylum, ready to begin her job. Alex, heading in the opposite direction, walked into the room which she had just exited from, and announced, "Finally unpacked!"

"About time," Carrie shouted from their kitchen, which sat directly next door. Michael snored, his head in his hand while he sat at the table.

Thomas laughed, "We go through this kind of stuff all the time."

"Just not as excessive as this has been," Danielle explained to the actress.

"Oh God," Carrie sighed, "I don't think I can handle this."

"It's pretty tough," Aaron told her, "But it pays, trust me." A large smirk developed as he spoke those words.

Alex cut in, "You better believe it." He turned to Thomas, "It's about time I head back. I'm paying for this place by the hour," he trailed off.

"I under –" Thomas was interrupted.

Derrick Smith

"Out of my pocket nonetheless," Alex complained. "I still can't believe they made me pay for this on my own."

Thomas just stared at him. He hoped he was finally finished, "You done?"

Alex looked toward him, cracked a smile, "Yeah, I'm good." After a brief silence, he began again, "Anyway, we really need to get going."

"Like I was going to say before, that's quite -" again, he got cut off.

"You have everything you need right?" Alex asked.

Thomas took a breath. He knew he did not have a chance to get a word in edgewise. "Okay," he finally said after a long pause.

"Good, here, take this," Alex handed Thomas an oversized cell phone.

"Thanks," Thomas said after taking the phone from him. He thought it looked like a prototype cell phone of sorts. "Um, I have a cell phone. I can just take your number."

Alex laughed, "No, no." He gave him an 'Are you stupid' kind of look. "It's an emergency phone, see," he pointed to the phone. It only had six buttons on it; numbers one through three, a '911' button, a speaker phone button, and the power button.

Thomas looked confused, he turned to the rest of the crew for some help or at least someone that understood the phone that he held. "How do I use it?" he motioned to Alex to show him.

Alex snatched the phone, "Power button, obviously." He pointed to the on/off button, "Then my cell phone is number one, work phone number two, and the number three is empty." Alex showed him as he spoke. He guided his finger over each number. "This is the emergency

64

number," he pointed to the '911' button. "This will dial directly to the nearest police station. Then this, I'm sure you've seen before," Alex slid his finger over the speakerphone key. "This is the speaker phone button. I don't really think you'd need this at all," he scratched his head.

"That seems almost too easy," Thomas tried to laugh. "Thank you," he paused, "And thank you for updating this part of the asylum for us."

"We really do appreciate it," Danielle spoke up. The rest of the group agreed. They nodded their heads and chimed in thanking him.

Alex held up his hands, "No, thank you, all of you. I am very lucky to have found you." He smiled, "Stick with me, and I'll make you famous." Alex paused. He noticed the investigation crew growing anxious to get started, "I promise."

"And rich," Scott chimed in. "Don't forget rich," a devilish smirk grew around his neatly trimmed beard.

"Of course not," Alex shared the same expression. "Fame and fortune my friends, just keep that in the back of your minds."

As he turned, ready to head out, Alex turned and glanced back. Thomas had already spun around to gather his crew to get started. "About damn time," he muttered under his breath. Alex strolled out of the asylum, into the truck, and both he and the truck driver left down the unattended dirt road.

Derrick Smith

Chapter 5

NOW OR NEVER

"Alright guys, time to eat," Thomas announced from their bedroom.

Michael was still asleep at the kitchen table. Carrie nudged him, "Wake up Mike."

"Huh, what I miss?" Michael jumped with a start.

She let out a laugh, "A lot, not like it matters." The two of them moved away from the table to make room for the others.

The crew made their way into the kitchen very slowly. They were all beat after they pulled every crate and special effects prop from the 18-wheeler. "Let's check and see what they left us to eat." Danielle pried opened the tiny refrigerator. She sighed at the sight of microwavable food packages.

"Oh boy," Aaron yelled out, "Just what I wanted." He grabbed a small parcel and showed it to everyone. "Look how spoiled we are." He smiled for a second then tossed the box in the microwave.

"We've got enough for about a week," Robin pointed toward the tiny red and blue food containers. Some were filled with Chinese, some beef, some pastas, a mixture of everything. It seemed just a very low budget.

Thomas smiled; he clicked the 5:00 minute button on the microwave, "Better than Missouri."

"What happened in Missouri?" Carrie questioned.

Scott pushed through everyone. He attempted to grab some food out of the fridge. "Alex gave us dried food cans for three straight days." He turned toward the microwave with a box of cold food in his hand. "He was...well...is an asshole." Scott tossed the box in the second microwave, "He'll never change, cheap bastard."

"You really need to stop living in the past," Danielle blurted out, "Who really gives a crap?" She looked around the room for anyone at all to speak out against her; she hoped they wouldn't.

Michael yawned then asked, "Is there something between the two of you? You've been at each other's throats all day."

"Yeah," Scott smiled, "I took her boyfriend's precious job." He let out a slight chuckle.

Danielle grew intolerant of Scott; she lashed out with all her might, "Son of a bitch." She thrashed about wildly but only hit air. She felt a sudden tug on her midsection. "What the..." she began to question but trailed off as she looked behind her.

Aaron grabbed her and pulled back. "Okay, I'm not worth this much interest," he laughed at his own joke. "Come on babe," he pulled her back into the bedroom.

"I hate that piece of trash!"

"I know you do," Aaron began, "But we all have to stay in this place for some time..." He took a breath, "Man, you really know how to tire me out, and your clothes are still on." He tried to get her to smile but fell quite short of his goal. Danielle still frowned. "I have an idea," he shouted.

Danielle just stared at the floor, "What is it? Kill him and bury his body within these walls?"

"Um, not quite my —" Aaron was cut off as quickly as he began.

"That's too bad, because you know, that would have been a fantastic idea." Danielle seemed to be quite serious.

Shocked at her remark, Aaron bent down and kissed her forehead. "Come on now, think of the money." This brought a smile upon her face. "What I was going to suggest is that we begin our tours and say screw them all." Her smile grew wider. Aaron grabbed his camera from the nightstand. "Come on babe," he grabbed her hand, "Let's get started.

"No, let's make some money," she said with a gleam in her eye. "There's no time like the present." The couple made their way into the hallway, past Robin, who didn't even look up. Past her gadgets, and finally began their quest for the paranormal, or in Danielle's case, the money.

Back in the kitchen, after the excitement concluded, the rest of the crew sat down to eat their microwavable meals. The crew sat anywhere they could fit, the table, countertop, beds; Thomas even sat on the floor.

"I don't think I can live like this for long," Carrie told Michael.

He looked up from his dinner, "I don't know." He took a second to swallow the fork-full of food he was currently chewing, "For this kind of money…"

Carrie obviously understood, for she dropped the subject and dug into her food.

Thomas butt into their conversation. "Truthfully," the two actors looked down toward him from the table. "I absolutely hate this shit." He stuffed a spoonful of green, crusty, green beans down his throat, "I just grin and bear it."

"I didn't mean to offend you guys," Carrie pleaded. "I guess for the money we're all making, it's worth eating this slop." She too ate some of her packaged provisions.

Thomas finished his plastic platter of frozen food. "Ya know," he swallowed, "You have a good point."

She looked up, a little confused. "Excuse me? What point?"

Michael turned to her, "That this food is disgusting," he laughed.

Thomas shot them both a smile, "You said you couldn't do this for long." He stood from his leg-crossed position, "Why don't we start this movie tonight?" His voice rose as he made sure everyone heard him. "We could be out of here in what? Four days?" Thomas looked over to Scott who sat on the newly finished edge of the counter.

"I don't see why not," Scott agreed. "We can go start our intros before the sun falls for the night if you want," Scott suggested.

"Why not?" Thomas asked. "What do you guys think?" he glanced toward the actors.

They looked at each other than shrugged their shoulders, "Why not?" Michael repeated Thomas' question.

"Are we even doing anything yet?" Carrie asked, not sure what to expect.

"Abso-fuckin-lutely!" Scott proclaimed. "We've always wanted to place some of our own 'spooks' around our shooting sites."

Thomas chimed in, "And you'll fit perfectly into that position."

"Hey guys, I'm going to be setting our stuff around inside," Robin announced after she poked her head in the room. She ducked back out just as fast as she had rushed in.

Carrie burst out in a loud roar. "Well, that wasn't weird or anything," she continued to laugh.

"She was doing what everyone is supposed to do," Scott defended her in a harsh manner.

Carrie showed slight bewilderment. She looked over to Michael and he had the same puzzled expression. "Anytime any of us goes off on our own, we must tell the group so —" Thomas's explanation abruptly ended.

"So the rest of us know the house didn't eat you, or that an undead entity did not abduct us," Scott stated, plenty of sarcasm radiated throughout his voice.

Carrie tried not to laugh; she held it in the best she could but it suddenly escaped her. She looked shocked, "I'm sorry, I...I...I," the actress stammered.

Scott smiled, "You think I'm joking?"

She was confused, with no idea of what to do; Carrie sat in silence, almost in shock.

"Stop it Scott," Thomas finally intervened, he looked down to Carrie. "He's right, he's an idiot," he tried to calm her down. "But he is right." Carrie looked up to him as he knelt down to her. "Anytime anyone goes anywhere in a building like this on their own," Thomas began to explain, he turned toward Michael as well. "They must tell us that they are leaving and why."

Michael and Carrie looked on with wide eyes. "Just don't trail off and you'll have nothing to worry about," Aaron chimed in.

"It's really nothing to worry about," Danielle looked around. "There're plenty of us here. Like Thomas said, just don't go exploring."

The two actors just turned toward each other; their grim faces said it all. "I don't know if I can do this," Carrie blurted out, she finally broke the silence.

Michael grabbed her hand, "We'll be fine, this place isn't haunted remember." She looked at him with puppy dog eyes, ready to sob. "It's these guys that are going to do all the scaring," he paused. "Really, don't worry," he hugged her tightly; "I'll protect you." The two actors moved back to the bedroom slowly.

"Okay," Thomas was ready to direct everyone. "We'll split up and begin taping."

"Sounds like a plan," Aaron said. The rest of the group nodded and agreed.

Scott grabbed his expensive, European camera, "Why are we waiting around then?"

"Good question," Danielle walked toward Thomas, "How do you want to do this?" The two investigators walked to the bedroom to discuss their plan of action.

Scott and Aaron grabbed their maps; many areas of the maps were already circled or highlighted. The two actors walked back into the kitchen, even after the investigators demanded everyone to leave. They both sat back at the table, "I don't have a good feeling about this," Carrie repeated. She began to panic. The two cameramen just stared at her. They obviously knew she was not up for what the crew was about to begin.

"Calm down, they're going to kick you out," Michael pleaded with her. "We both need this money. You know?" Michael held her hand again, "Please."

Carrie took a deep breath, "Okay, okay." She continued to take deep breaths.

Thomas and Danielle re-entered the room. "Alright guys," Thomas bellowed, "we're splitting up into groups."

Danielle spoke up, "It's going to be Aaron and myself, Thomas and Scott, and the two of you," she pointed toward the actors. "You'll be helping Robin set everything up."

Carrie looked toward the leaders; she was about to ask them why they chose those groups. Before she could even ask her question, the four team members picked up their maps, cameras, and flashlights and headed out the door.

Michael tugged at her arm. "Come on," he begged her. "We've got to go find Robin." She finally budged, "Remember what Thomas told us?" He waited for a response. When she said nothing, Michael continued, "We cannot get lost, we need to stick with someone." Carrie bobbed her head; she realized she didn't have much choice.

While the pair left, the four others prepared themselves for the first step into their sham of a movie. Thomas and Scott headed toward the front gates, in order to gain their opening shot. Danielle and Aaron, on the other hand, journeyed to the cemetery so the co-star could fake her way through her supposed psychic experience. They dispersed without a word, aside from Thomas' command, "We will all meet back in one hour; right before the sun goes down. Hopefully Alex will have the generators running at that point." They split up as they attempted to gain as much footage as possible on the first night.

As Carrie and Michael navigated down the treacherous hallway, they crawled over crates, around human-like dummies, and even under hanging wires. Both performers thought the same thing: *There is no way this will be finished in time.* The darkness approached, the shadows began to fall along the already dimly lit walls.

"We better find her before this place hits complete darkness," Carrie warned. She kept her eyes on Michael for reassurance that everything would be fine, just like he said.

He called out repeatedly, "Robin!" To no avail, they could not find her anywhere. "Where is she?" he questioned under his breath.

The pair continued down the hall. They passed abandoned, foul rooms. Each individual space seemed to carry its own aura or vibe. It felt as if they held their own horror stories and past life-lines. Carrie began to feel as if someone was watching them, almost like a pair of eyes gleamed through each door they passed.

"Snap out of it," Michael grabbed her arm. "Come on, we don't have to stay long, just do what they ask."

Carrie's eyes grew wide with shock and fear. "Okay," she recollected her thoughts and attitude. "Robin!" her voice cracked. She continued to feel the presence all around her, almost as if a shadowy figure stalked them

A loud scratch noise echoed down the hall, the two actors turned immediately. "What was that?" Carrie asked quickly.

Michael just stared into the darkness. "Robin!" he began to raise his voice. They broke off into a slow sprint toward the entrance of the building where Robin housed most of her equipment.

Whispers ricocheted throughout the building now, from inside broken-down patients rooms, to as far as the pair could hear. Many different whispers came and went, just as fast as they appeared. "Okay, this is really messed up," Carrie howled.

"You aren't kidding," announced Michael. "I'm getting really freaked out right now." They kept moving, not as if they had a choice, all the other crew members took off in different directions.

A shadowy figure lurked behind them; Carrie just knew it. She kept her head cocked to the side; she was sure she saw something. A sudden gust of wind blew behind the pair. They both swung around quickly.

Michael gasped; he glanced at the wall; there were thick patches of some sort of liquid.

"No," Michael uttered, "No way." He pointed to the wall. "What is that?" he stammered.

Carrie drew close to it and touched it hesitantly. She rubbed her fingers together; she gasped and rubbed her hands on her shirt immediately. "It can't be," she jumped back to Michael, "Blood."

A hand grabbed Michael's shoulder, he let out a shrill scream and jumped backward, he crashed into Carrie as the two flew back, and they hit the wall. It gave way, both actors collapsed through the wall and landed on top of each other.

As they departed from the rest of the crew, Aaron and Danielle made their way toward the chapel. The chapel sat in the rear of the building, directly across from the violent wing of the building. "Grab the camera, babe," Danielle commanded Aaron.

He grabbed his camera and lifted it up to his shoulder, "You ready with your story?"

"What do you think?" she asked with sarcasm. "I'm always ready."

Aaron laughed, "Yeah, yeah, you're always right." He held his hand up, the camera light flashed on. He counted down with his fingers, three...two...one...he pointed toward Danielle.

Danielle began, "As you can see, the chapel is one of the very few places in this nearly one hundred-year-old building that is left mainly intact." She walked toward the oak finished doors; Aaron followed closely. "The hospital was rebuilt and updated nearly ten different times. This is the only original, self-sustained area in this building. Originally, it was detached from the hospital."

She pushed open the door with a loud groan, the sound echoed throughout the chapel and the building alike. "Eventually, with the addition of more and more patients, the building was extended to this point and connected." She waved her arm in the air, "Luckily there is still a little light remaining so you can see the beautiful stained-glass windows. This is not the largest of churches, but in the case of a mental institution, was very overused." There were about ten pews total in the building.

They both walked deeper into the church, deeper into the darkness, "The public knew somewhat, but not too much about this place; just enough to concern themselves with the reputation. After they learned that patients were dying frequently, the community got involved." The two crew members reached the front pew; Danielle sat, and continued "They had an inspector make surprise visits at their will. It was learned that the doctors were operating on the patients with new techniques, some were considered brutal and inhumane." She rose and walked further toward the shadows.

"After that incident, the doctors began hiding their experiments and new methods of research, such as drugs to boost brain functions, calm patients down, or even put them to sleep, sometimes for good." Danielle paused for a long period of time, "Turn it off."

Aaron put the camera down, "Everything alright?"

Danielle looked up to him, tears grew in her eyes. "I'm fine," her voice cracked. "It's just, just…"

"I know it's tough," Aaron pleaded, "This is where your grandfather passed away."

"It's fine," she bellowed, "That's all in the past. How'd it sound?"

Aaron smiled, he picked up his camera once again, "Amazing, simply and utterly amazing!"

A loud crash reverberated from behind the altar. The pair jumped and spun around. Out of pure fear, they began to run for the door. "Turn the camera on!" Danielle screamed.

Aaron looked stunned but understood; he turned it on and whirled back to face the unknown perpetrator. Danielle continued to the door, "It seems as though we awoke a spirit from a past life." Out of breath, she tried to continue, "Maybe it's one of the doctors who went insane and died here from starvation." She ventured back into the room after the initial shock wore off, "Please, do not harm us; we are only here to help."

They both moved toward the area from where the sound echoed. "If you have a message to bring to us from the afterlife, you may do so now," Danielle explained. The doors immediately slammed shut, again they both circled toward the noise.

"Okay," Aaron stuttered, "I'm getting kind of freaked out." He backed off, he tripped over the altar. "Shit, look," he pointed behind the altar.

Danielle rushed over; she kept her eye on the doors. "Oh," she was taken back. Aaron had uncovered the original sound; the podium had toppled over. Not just the podium however, the bible had been torn to shreds and a body lay underneath it. "Come on, help me!" Danielle shouted.

Aaron hustled over to the podium to help lift it, suddenly the gigantic cross collapsed on top of the podium; it completely crushed the remains of the body under it. "No!" Aaron cried out. Both crew members dashed to the flattened body.

"Help!" Danielle cried out, "Please, someone!"

Aaron lurched himself up off the ground, "We have to go find Tommy. He has the only working phone in this dump."

Tears began to stream down her face, "Alright," Danielle stammered. Aaron helped her to her feet. "I don't know how much of this I can take," she wiped blood off of her hands onto her jeans.

The couple moved swiftly toward the closed doors, "Let's hope they're not locked," Aaron held her tightly. He pulled the handle hard; the door gave way only slightly but opened regardless. Upon opening the door the two crew members stepped back, mouths agape. A figure stood in the gloomy hallway, about twenty feet away from the chapel.

"Hello? Who's there?" Danielle still had a little stutter in her voice from the shock.

Aaron stepped in front of Danielle, "Scott, is that you?"

Silence.

"Robin?"

The figure just stood still in the darkness. It was tall, shrouded in a black sweatshirt, hood pulled halfway over its face. The unknown figure finally stepped forward and began to laugh. Its voice was shrill and echoed throughout the hall.

"Danielle, stay behind me," Aaron nudged her behind him. She looked up to him with glassy eyes. "It'll be okay."

The figure drew closer with every step, "What do you think you're doing?" Another laugh bellowed from the shrouded figure.

"What do you want?" Aaron demanded.

No answer, the figure moved closer to the light; and to the two of them.

Aaron took a step back, had an arm on Danielle, "Stay back; I don't know what's going to happen." Aaron stood ready on guard, as if he was about to fight off an attacker.

Danielle took a few steps back, not sure how to react. She stood in the doorway of the chapel as the figure came closer, and closer, and closer.

The two actors lay inside of the ominous room; the only light that shone through was from the hole they created in the wall. Michael began to stir.

"Carrie!" he shouted, she did not even twitch. "Are you alright?" Carrie was positioned on her side, completely motionless. He shook her, "Carrie, wake up!" Darkness almost completely surrounded them. Michael looked up to the hole that now led to the hallway.

His eyes were blurry, most likely caused by the fall onto the hard concrete floor. As his eyes focused, he noticed two dark silhouettes directly opposite of the hole. Barely any light drew past them into the room. "Hello?" He tried to make his way to his feet. "Who's there?"

The figures glared into the hole; two red eyes appeared as they drew closer. Light had practically vanished from the room, the two bodies stood inside the room directly in front of the hole.

"Please. No!" Michael stammered. "Carrie, Carrie!" She began to awaken. "Come on, we have to go!" He was in a crouched position; he tried to lift Carrie to her feet.

"Wh-what?" she asked with a glazed-over look in her eyes. "Where are-"

"Someone is after us. Let's go!" He dragged her to feet after a moment of resistance. "Come on!"

The two actors raced into the darkness, they tripped over chairs, trays, and their own feet. There was no chance anyone could see where they were so Michael grabbed for Carrie and pulled her back.

"Stop, I think we lost them," he whispered, although practically out of breath.

Carrie tried to pull away, "No, they'll get us, I know they will!"

"Come on Carrie," he tried to calm her down again. "There's no way –"

Suddenly there was a loud crash, "What the hell?" Michael jumped. "Okay," he thought for a second, "maybe we should keep moving."

They moved further into the darkness, there seemed to be nothing in front of them. Michael turned back and saw two red eyes move toward them once again. "No," he screamed, "stay away!"

Carrie turned back toward the light, "Oh God; no." She leaned in toward Michael, "We've hit a wall."

"What do you want?" he demanded, "Please, we'll give you whatever you want!"

Nothing.

Carrie pushed her back against the wall as hard as she could; she hoped to break through another wall as easily as the original had given way. She couldn't budge it, *I'm a fool,* she thought. "You just want our reactions don't you?" She took a step forward, she almost tripped over Michael. "Worthless pieces of shit!" she screeched at the lights.

They turned off all of a sudden. Carrie smirked, "I knew it."

Michael was backed into the corner, cradled in the fetal position. He didn't say a word or make a sound. He was nearly in shock.

"Michael?" Carrie bent over to him; she felt around for his hand. It was cold as ice. She shook him, "Michael, snap out of it." Carrie began to panic; she peered over her shoulder for the lights. "Hello?" She shuttered

Nothing.

"Mike, please, wake up."

Another loud noise echoed throughout the room. Then a masculine voice, "Shit!"

"Are you alright?" a feminine voice asked.

The manly voice replied, "I'm fine, that just really hurt."

"Help me, there's something wrong with him," she pointed down toward Michael.

A light flashed on suddenly, it blinded Carrie as Michael still stared into nothingness. Carrie threw her arms in the air; she tried to dim the bright light.

"God, what's your problem?" Carrie grew impatient. "Who's there? You need to help." Once again she pointed toward Michael, this time she grabbed his hand. "You'll be fine," she comforted him.

"Okay, cameras off!" the female voice commanded. "That's gone far enough."

Carrie stood, still dazed, "This was all your idea?" She ran over to the two bodies and smacked them. She was still partially blinded but didn't care. "You did this? Why would you do this?" she demanded. "Bastards!" Carrie pulled her arm back, ready for another blow when someone grabbed her wrist.

"This is your job," the voice explained. "I realize a lot of abnormal crap can happen in a place like this, but you signed on for it."

Carrie stood dumbfounded; she finally fixed her eyes upon the entity. It was Scott and, standing beside him, was Robin. "How'd you get here?" she asked. "You were behind us." Carrie motioned backward.

"It doesn't matter, we need to get him out of here," Robin exclaimed. She bent over to him; the darkness owned the room once again. "I can't see anything. Scott, can you -?" She was cut off as a ray of light shone through the thick darkness.

Scott had clicked on a small flashlight. "I'm a step ahead of you," he winked at her, although she ignored it.

Carrie stood back, still concerned for Michael as well as angry that they pulled that stunt. "Why did you try to harm us?" she asked once again.

"One...two...three," Scott counted. On three, he and Robin lifted Michael. He was practically brain dead at this point. "Is it even worth dragging him all that way back?"

"You piece of shit," Carrie tried to swing at him again. Scott ducked and nearly lost his grip on Michael. Robin grabbed Carrie's arm with her free hand.

"Okay, Car, it's alright. He's just naturally a jerk," Robin explained to her as blatantly as possible. She looked to Scott, "You really don't have to be such a fool."

A smile grew on Scott's face, "It's natural and besides," he paused as he tried to get a good grip on Michael, "it's my hobby."

"You're an imbecile," Carrie nearly screamed at him, then held herself back. She glanced toward Robin, "Can we please get him back to the bedroom?"

Robin nodded, "Yes, come on, Scott, let's go."

"Yesa masa," Scott sarcastically replied. He took a second to gather his thoughts, "It is getting dark and the damn lights that Alex promised would be working by dawn still haven't been turned on!"

The three of them made their way back up the hallway from where they had ventured, they took turns as they dragged Michael, who was only half conscious, back with them. Scott and Robin bickered relentlessly, and Carrie tried to hold her tears back. This was all just too much for her.

The figure stopped dead in its tracks. Still in the darkness, the two team members were unable to identify who, or what, the figure was. It was dressed all in black, that they could tell for sure, and the face was white. As pale as a corpse, and resembling a human skull, the figure's face was solemn; it did not make a sound or move a muscle.

Suddenly, the door slammed shut. Danielle and Aaron jumped back as the large, oak double doors nearly crushed both of them. After the initial shock of the doors crash, they both attempted to push them back open out of pure curiosity of the figure's identity.

"No luck," Aaron announced, "something is keeping them closed."

Danielle kicked and beat the door repeatedly, "What happened? No one else was out there…were they?"

He just shook his head, somewhat wearily. "There was a man – or uh something right there. I want to know who was doing that, because it's not funny."

"Everything we do is planned out; no one should have been there." Danielle began to shake, "I'm scared," her voice cracked.

Aaron wrapped his arm around her, "It'll be okay. I do want to know who that was though." He continued to try to pry open the door.

"There's no way we're going to get back –"

A hand had reached out from the darkness and grabbed her shoulder and tried to pull her into the darkness. Danielle shrieked and leapt back in terror.

Aaron swung around, "What the –" He grabbed her hand and tugged back as hard as he could. "No, Danielle!"

"Help me!" she bellowed, tears streamed down her cheeks.

"Stop!" a voice commanded.

Danielle continued to struggle, "Let go...of...me!" At her command, she went flying on top of Aaron and they both crashed against the door.

"It's me, it's me, stop!" a voice groaned from the darkness.

"Tom? Is that you?" Aaron asked in astonishment.

A man grew closer to them, "Yes, yes! Damn Danielle, I think you bruised a rib or two."

She tried to pull herself from her fear, "What do you expect? I thought I was being taken by the house!"

Both men let out a laugh, "Um, I don't know what planet you just came from, but after everything that we have done, have you ever seen anything truly paranormal?" Thomas asked sarcastically.

"Okay, enough Tom, please," Aaron glanced up toward Thomas. "I was scared out of my mind too. I really didn't know what was going on."

"Alright," Thomas laughed again. "You guys did well though, I must say."

Danielle and Aaron looked at each other quickly. "What do you mean? Was all this set up?" Danielle asked, extremely frustrated. She pointed to the altar, "And that man? He is fake, right?"

"Yes," Thomas looked to the altar and up at the doors, "Robin planned out this room. She's pretty good, isn't she?"

"I got to admit, she had me believing," Aaron explained. "So, the door too?"

Thomas pointed up to the top hinge with his camera light, "Look closely." There were two very tiny air compressed tension springs. "I have this little…thing," he held up a small remote, which obviously controlled the doors to swing one way or another.

"That's amazing," Danielle was still in some shock.

Aaron stepped back beside Danielle, "You know what really amazes me?" He paused to see Thomas' expression, "How you were able to make it from out there to in here."

Thomas, apparently confused, shook his head and simply asked, "What?"

"You know," Danielle reaffirmed Aaron's question, "how you got in here, I mean there are no other entrances are there? Maybe an underground tunnel by chance?" She nudged Aaron and a smirk grew upon his face.

"That must be it, huh? A tunnel from the hallway somewhere to in here behind us, right" Aaron seemed eager.

Thomas once again shook his head and ran his fingers through his thick, black hair, "There is a tunnel over by the altar but that leads outside to the woods. There used to be a creek back there I think."

"Wait, wait," Aaron held up his hands, "you're saying that that figure out there wasn't you?"

"Nope, I've been in here, sort of lurking around so I could film you guys unnoticed." He showed a little concern now. "You seriously saw someone else in here?"

Danielle's fear seemed to creep back upon her, "Yes, there was definitely a man out there, he was all black, and, and..." she nervously drew a blank.

"His face was very pale and seemed to resemble a, um, skull..." Aaron trailed off in confusion.

Thomas showed slight disbelief, "Alright, if there was someone out there, maybe what a kid? We'll find him." He clicked his remote's button and reopened the doors. "Shall we?"

Danielle looked up to Aaron, "Can we just go back?"

Aaron put his arms around her again, "Yeah, Tom, can we just head back to the more modernized wing?"

After a sigh, Thomas replied, "I suppose, besides, the lights still haven't turned on and we won't be able to see anything in here after the sun fully goes down."

"Thank you, thank you," Aaron was very gracious for his decision. He stretched his arms around her tall, slender body and gave Danielle a long hug then reached for her hand.

Thomas walked out of the chapel into the hallway in front of the small group. He shone his camera's bright light down the hall. "This way guys, follow me."

The three ventured back into the darkness from where they came. The comfort of light, heat, and food was their motivation; aside from the apparent relief of the figure that both Danielle and Aaron had encountered.

Derrick Smith

Chapter 6

CHANGING ROLES

The darkness had consumed the narrow hallways of the seemingly evil asylum. Doors slammed, floors creaked, even bats fluttered above the new inmates' heads. On their journey back to their safe haven, Thomas, Danielle, and Aaron climbed over and under, in and out, any way imaginable in order to avoid all obstacles that set in their way; both Robin's creative booby traps and previous asylum foliage. By the time the three reached the door of their updated room, they were all bent over, out of breath.

"Dear God," Danielle breathed heavily, "that took forever and a half."

Aaron stood up, hands on his hips. "That took so much longer coming back than it was on the way to the chapel." He tried to show that he wasn't tired but suddenly bent back over to suck in more deep breaths.

"Can we finally sit down and take a breath?" Danielle asked a little perturbed.

"Absolutely, I'm done running from imaginary spooks!" Thomas exclaimed sarcastically. After a brief pause, he finally opened the door, allowing himself to regain his energy. He was followed by Aaron and Danielle, hand in hand. After they took only a single step into the room, the three stopped suddenly, all stared wide-eyed.

"Wh-what the hell?" Aaron stammered. He stared blankly at the bed which detained a crazed actor.

Danielle took a step forward and put a hand on Carrie's shoulder who sat next to the bed, tears streamed down her cheeks. "What happened to him?" His wrists were bloody as though a creature clawed at them. Restraints wrapped under the bed and pinned his wrists to the aged mattress.

Carrie didn't say a word; she stared at Michael then laid her head in her hands. Danielle looked up toward Aaron and the still speechless Thomas. "What do we do?"

Both men shrugged their shoulders and finally made their way into the room. Robin stepped in from the kitchen area. "I don't know," she began, "we practically drug him back from one of the violent patient hallways. As soon as we saw the light from our room, he just freaked out." She looked down to Michael.

"What do you mean freaked out?" Danielle asked. "This looks a little bit more than some spasm or something."

Carrie stood and pulled her shirt collar to her shoulder. "This, for one," she pointed to the large, red, hand imprint left on her neck. Deep scratches were also burrowed into her shoulder, most likely created from Michael's fingernails.

"He attacked you?" Aaron asked as his voice trembled.

Robin gave Carrie a frozen container of peas, "I guess you could say that."

"You guess?" Thomas finally chimed in, "How can you guess? That looks quite precise."

"Well, it's not as if he just up and jumped me," Carrie placed her hand on Michael's. "He sort of, well, I don't really know. He started shaking and growling, then got very feisty."

Robin walked back into the kitchen, "That's probably the best way to describe it. It's as if something triggered a…a…transformation."

"The light," Thomas murmured.

"What?" Danielle questioned. "How could light cause a transformation?" she asked very sarcastically.

Thomas blew out a sigh, "I don't know, but we have seen some pretty messed up stuff."

"Well, whatever caused it, it's nothing good," Robin paused to gather her thoughts. "We were able to restrain him, well, it was mostly Scott. We used some of our belts and one of the straps from that wheelchair out in the hall," she pointed out the door.

Thomas walked over to Michael. He bent down and just stared impassively into Michael's eyes. He muttered something under his breath then just drew closer.

"What'd you say?" Robin asked.

Danielle and Aaron both drew closer. "Nooo! Let me out. Fuck you all! Let me out, I don't belong here!" Michael growled. He almost seemed possessed and began to shout in different languages. One of the straps broke loose; Michael grabbed Thomas as he tried to jump out of his range. Thomas felt himself pulled toward the monster on the bed. "Release me. Get me out of here," Michael's voice became deep and scratchy.

Thomas didn't say a word; he nearly went into shock from the fear. When Michael did not receive a reply from the mastermind of the operation, he grabbed Thomas' collar with his sole free hand and tossed him over the bed, against a wall; which in turn cracked upon the impact. Thomas' brawny body sank to the floor without so much of a scream of pain.

"Grab him!" Robin screamed at Aaron.

Aaron grabbed Michael's arm and pinned it to the mattress. Danielle pulled off Aaron's belt and wrapped it around the bedpost and tied it tight around Michael's arm. The couple fell back against the door in a tired heap.

"Dear God," Carrie sobbed, "is he possessed?" She fell back into her position beside the bed, and she began to pray.

Aaron pulled himself up, "I need a drink."

"I hear that," Danielle followed him to Thomas.

"Come on buddy," Aaron pulled Thomas to his feet.

Robin walked over to the trio and put an arm around Thomas, "Come on, let's grab you an ice pack...well a bag of peas," she joked.

Thomas didn't flinch, "Where is Scott anyway?"

"Well, nothing can turn *you* away from this job, can it?" again Robin tried to make Thomas smile.

Thomas rubbed his shoulder, "I just think we need to take a little more precaution, I mean this house may have a little more to offer than just a good setting."

"What? You mean like it's actually haunted?" Aaron smirked. "After everything we've been through, I just don't think I believe in that crap anymore."

Thomas shrugged off Aaron's arrogance, "Robin, where is Scott?"

Robin stared at Michael as he tried to squirm his way out of his restraints. More blood drew from his forearms as the straps dug into his flesh. She didn't say a word, simply pointed to the door. Everyone's faces became pale in disbelief.

"Not smart," Carrie announced as if no one else agreed. "We shouldn't be here, look what happened to Mike, not here, no, not here." She went back to her prayer beside the bed.

Danielle and Aaron proceeded to the kitchen to retrieve their drinks. Neither spoke a word after hearing what Carrie had to say. Thomas and Robin just stared at each other for a moment then back down to Michael. "We need to get this done, and quickly," Thomas spoke very softly to Robin.

All of a sudden, a bright light shone through the cracks in the door. "I told you," Carrie shouted. "Look, they've come for us! They're here to finish the job!"

Aaron and Danielle ran back into the room, each carried a beer. "Are you insane? Do you even know…?" Aaron trailed off and shook his head in sheer amazement.

Robin leaned in toward Thomas, "What should we do?"

"Pray," Carrie cut in, "it's all we can do."

"She might be right," Danielle announced, somewhat in shock.

Aaron grabbed her tight and whispered, "Don't listen to her, she's scared out of her mind, and probably a little crazy on top of it."

Danielle looked up to him and gave him a very gentle gaze.

Thomas stared at the door, wide-eyed, he didn't say a word. He began to step backward, into the kitchen. The others followed him; no one knew what to do or how to react. The four petrified investigators hit the farthest wall in the kitchen as they left Carrie and Michael in front of the bright, white-outlined door.

"Carrie!" Robin shouted, "Come in here!"

She didn't even look up, too heavily entrenched in prayer.

Aaron picked up a kitchen chair, "We need to get out of here!" He pulled the chair back and slammed it against the kitchen wall. The chair burst into a hundred shards of splintered lumber.

"These walls are nothing like the rest of the asylum," Thomas explained, "these have been reinforced by Max's contractors with steel."

They all looked back toward the door as it began to shake violently. The doorknob turned ever so slowly.

"What do we do?" Robin once again begged.

Thomas continued to stare at the light beams which shone around the door, "What can we do?"

The door swung open; a black silhouette was outlined as the light shone behind it. The group joined close together in the kitchen while Carrie held Michael's now squirming hand.

"Oh, God," Danielle pleaded, "Please help us!"

"Jesus!" the silhouetted figure shouted. "I think I'm blind!" A deep laugh echoed through the room.

Danielle stepped forward, "Scott?"

"Man, those lights are ridiculous," Scott said. "I got a ton of awesome footage until those damn lights burned my retinas."

"You scared the piss out of all of us," Robin slapped Scott repeatedly on his chest as she inched forward. "How could you do that?"

After faltering backward, Scott grabbed her. "What are you talking about? I was on my way back and the lights turned on out of nowhere. What, you think I turned on the lights to scare you?"

"Well, it sure seemed like –" Danielle was cut off.

"It doesn't matter," Thomas arguably interfered, "we just really need to hurry everything up and get the hell out of here!"

Scott looked around, "What are you talking about, that whole Michael thing was just some breakdown. You all worry too much."

The emergency cell phone rang very loudly, repeatedly.

Scott pointed to a large, black duffel bag which sat in a pile of luggage. "You going to get that?"

Thomas made his way over to the pile and dug around. The phone was near the bottom of his bag, "Hello?"

"Thomas? Is that you?" the voice asked on the other side of the phone.

Thomas paused, wondering why he had to ask, "Yea, Max, it's me. I see you got the lights working."

A thunderous laugh bellowed through the ear piece, "Yea, I'm sure it's bright for now but just give it time, they sort of have to warm up then cool back down."

"Works for us, thank you."

Carrie ran over to Thomas, "Tell him about Mike, tell him what happened, tell him we need help," Carrie demanded. She tried to get Max to hear on the other side, "Why won't you tell him? Please, you must!"

Danielle nudged Aaron; he ran over to Carrie and covered her mouth. "Shh, quiet," he beckoned.

Carrie fought and squirmed but to no avail. Her screams muffled but her body language showed her frustrations.

"Is everything alright so far, Tommy?" Max asked after he heard the screams.

Thomas turned away from Carrie and waved his hand to try to get her to quiet down, "Yea, yea, all is good. That's just Robin testing some of her equipment." He turned toward Carrie and shot her a quick smirk.

The team members kept quiet, Aaron restrained Carrie, and Michael lay motionless on the aged mattress as Thomas assured that all was perfectly fine.

"Just make sure you guys take your time, this will be perfect," Max advised.

Thomas smiled again, "Oh, it will be, I'll bet my soul on it."

"Make me proud," Alex declared. The phone went dead.

"Come on everyone, we need to –" Thomas once again was cut off.

Carrie broke away from Aaron's grasp and sprinted toward Thomas. "Why didn't you tell him? We need to get out of here, it's not safe! We...oof!"

Danielle punched her right in the gut, "You don't get it do you?" Everyone looked on in awe. "If that man, no, that monster finds out what happened," she chuckled, "he'll pull us all off this and find a new crew for even less money."

Carrie looked up as she tried to pull herself to her feet by means of Danielle's pant leg. "But he needs help, don't you see?"

"Yes," Scott interrupted. "I think we all see a very screwed up, crazy bitch."

"Enough!" Thomas shouted. "Let's get down to business. We need to start some of our story lines so we can get the hell out of here." The group stood silent. "Carrie," she looked up from the ground, a little startled.

"Yes?"

"Can you perform?" Thomas asked in a very stern tone.

She seemed to be deep in thought, "I think –"

"Are you sure that's a good idea?" Danielle asked. Aaron grabbed her arm as if to tell her to keep quiet.

Thomas stared at her, "At this point, it doesn't matter. We just need to finish this. She was hired to do a job. And by God," he turned his attention toward Carrie, "she's going to do it."

"Actually," Carrie looked up with wide, puppy-dog eyes, "I don't know if I can right now."

Aaron grabbed Danielle's hand, "Come on babe. Let's get some sleep." He was stopped in his tracks as Danielle tugged on his hand, "Danny?"

"Tommy," Danielle looked back at Aaron, "I'll take her place."

Aaron shot her an irritated glance, "Are you kidding? Let the crazy lady do her job!"

"Whoa, calm down there Johnny hotcakes," Scott barked.

Robin giggled, "Okay, so we got our next shot, can we please get this shot done? I'm tired as all hell."

"Thank you, Tom," Carrie thankfully announced.

He gave her a soft smile then turned away, "Come on guys, off to the lab." Thomas turned to the door and turned the doorknob. "Carrie, are you okay to stay here with Mike?"

She nodded her head, "I think I should stay with him." Carrie walked back to his bed and reclaimed her position at his side. By now, the sleeping pills that Scott had given Michael to sleep had kicked in. He was out like a light.

"Alright guys," Thomas looked around, "let's get going. I want to get some sleep tonight."

He exited their haven and entered the now bright hallway. Robin, Danielle, Aaron, and Scott followed just a stride behind him, all ready to begin the next segment.

"Here we are," Thomas pointed toward the aged, deteriorating sign on the door that read 'Laboratory'. The group stared in silence.

Robin stepped forward, "Shall we?" She nudged the door open, "Wait till you see my chair," she grinned.

"Are there lights in here by chance?" Scott was hesitant to enter. "Wait, wait, you have a…chair," Scott mocked her.

Robin reached out and heaved a switch upward, "Just one." One sole light flashed on, "And yes, a chair."

"Oh," Scott stared in awe.

A single, steel, rusty chair sat in the center of the lab. It was reminiscent of an electric chair, equipped with wrist and ankle straps, an electric voltage box, and head harness attached roughly eight inches about the chair.

"This," Robin strolled into the room and pointed to the revolting fixture, "is my chair." She wandered toward it, slid her hands over its rough surface, over the arms, across the back, and finally came full circle around her contraption. "I know, it looks crude," as she sat in it, only to be cut off.

"I wouldn't sit in that thing if my life depended on it," Scott scoffed. "Good luck, Danny."

Aaron gave Scott a dirty look and shoved him with his shoulder as he passed, "Um, yeah, I don't know about –" Danielle's elbow struck him, "Oof!"

She stepped forward, toward Aaron, "I'm a big girl, I can take care of myself," she informed him, and then turned back toward Robin.

"As I was saying, "Robin proceeded, "It's actually brand new and constructed very well. I just crafted it to look old and dingy."

Thomas allowed a smile to show through, "You did a marvelous job, Robin." He walked over to join Robin at the chair and placed a hand on her shoulder, "Very impressive."

Robin's rosy cheeks flushed, even more than usual, but no one really noticed due to the dim lighting.

"So, what exactly does she need to do?" Aaron once again spoke for Danielle.

"Aaron!" Danielle roared. "Stop it!"

"Okay," Thomas broke in, "all you really need to do is sit in Robin's chair." He sat Robin down to demonstrate. "See," Thomas strapped Robin's wrists and ankles then placed the metal bowl-looking object on her head. "At this point, we will all leave, you'll scream, then we'll bust in the door to 'rescue' you."

Danielle seemingly grew anxious; chills crawled up her back, "Just scream?"

"Three times," Scott stepped forward and held up three fingers.

"Huh?" Danielle looked up to Scott then back to Thomas. "Just scream?" she asked again.

"We'll leave. I'll yell *go*, and you scream as loud as you can. Pause, and then scream once more. That's when we'll come in and you'll scream one last time."

"Simple enough," Danielle nodded her head. Aaron attempted to wrap his arms around her but she pushed away.

Thomas continued, "Yeah, plus it shouldn't take all that long."

"So we can get some damn sleep," Scott yawned in the process.

Danielle shot him an annoyed look, "Do you always need to be so crude?"

"Yeah man, is that really necessary?" Aaron once again butted in.

Danielle turned to Aaron and pushed him. He took a step back from the blow. "Seriously Aaron. Stop!"

Aaron looked dumbfounded, "Stop what?"

"You know what!" Danielle grumbled.

"Backing you up?"

"No, pushing my buttons. You know exactly how to piss me off and you never stop!"

Scott chuckled.

Aaron snapped at Scott, "Shut the hell up." He pulled his arm back and made a fist. He thrust forward; Danielle jumped in the way. He tried to hold back but could only change direction.

"Wha…" Robin, who had begun to exit the chair, slammed to the ground as Aaron's fist smashed into her cheek. She fell awkwardly due to her arm still trapped in one of the cuffs.

Thomas and Scott rushed forward and grabbed both of Aaron's arms. "What is your problem?" Scott demanded.

"You were…I didn't…It was an accident," Aaron stammered.

"Why don't you just go back to the room with Carrie?" Thomas forcefully asked.

Scott shoved Aaron out the door. "Come on dude, you messed up once already," Scott pleaded as Aaron fought back. "You really want to do it again?"

Aaron discontinued his futile attempt to return to his girlfriend and simply lowered his head. "I was just trying to be nice," he sobbed to Danielle. Aaron finally turned to leave, but once more turned back. "I'm sorry."

Danielle turned her back to him, "I'm really sorry Robin." She had begun to walk toward her and Thomas.

"Why don't we get this started finally so we can call it a night?" Thomas suggested as he held a small rag to Robin's lip. "Way too much has happened already."

"Good call," Scott chimed in, "I'm tired as hell!"

Robin pulled her shirt up to her lip after the rag filled with her blood, "It's so cold." She shivered as she lowered her shirt.

"Danielle," Thomas beckoned her, "if you don't mind." He guided her to the chair.

Danielle made her way over to the chair very slowly. She began to think this whole setup was a bad idea. "This won't take long, right?" she too began to tremble, "I don't like being alone in the dark."

"No, just a minute or two," Thomas encouraged her.

Robin reached for her hand. "Remember," she pointed up to the ceiling at a small, black object, "there are cameras everywhere. We'll be able to see you, there's nothing to be afraid of."

Danielle nodded her head in agreement while Thomas strapped her in. On the other side of the room, Scott shifted from side to side in order to find good camera angles.

"Ready?" Thomas asked.

Still too frightened to speak, Danielle simply nodded her head once more.

Robin once again grabbed her hand, "Really, do not worry," she gave Danielle a warm, reassuring smile.

"Okay, remember," Thomas explained, "scream twice after we say go - "

"Then once again when we burst in," Scott cut in. "I think she's got it."

Thomas once again tried to explain, "Give us about a minute or two before we start. I'll yell go."

Danielle understood, "Okay."

Thomas motioned to the crew out the door; he was the last to leave. "See you in a few," he winked as he stepped into the bright hallway.

Danielle sat in the chair, near panic. She waited for what seemed like hours until Thomas shouted, "Go!"

She screamed twice as loud as she could, but not for the movie. She was in sheer pain.

The lights blew out as the door slammed open. Danielle continued to scream. "Help, please!" The screams continued as they echoed into the hallway, and reverberated throughout the entire building.

"This is fantastic," Scott whispered. *Who needs actors*, he thought to himself.

The only light that shone in the room now was the camera light. As it pointed toward Danielle, the crew stopped dead in its tracks.

"What the...?" Robin trailed off.

A horrific scene lay before them. Two needles stuck in Danielle's arms. Blood seeped from each protrusion and puddles formed on the concrete beneath her. More dark red blood spilled from behind her eyes, then dripped down to her shirt which was already covered in blood. Her body convulsed as though she had been given shock therapy, her arms twitched in the wrist cuffs, her legs kicked violently, her head shook so rapidly the chair nearly gave way.

Thomas stumbled forward and began to unbuckle her with the help of Robin. "What the hell happened?" Thomas shouted.

"I have no idea; we were only out there for a few minutes!" Robin seemed just as confused.

Scott could not move nor speak, so he continued to do what he was hired to do, film.

"Turn some fuckin' lights on Robin; we got to get her out of here!" Thomas commanded.

"We...I...I..." she stammered.

The duo finally broke Danielle free of her restraints. "Danny! Danny!" Thomas hollered. "Stay with me!" Her eyes rolled to the back of her head. "Scott! Dial 911!"

Scott did not answer, he just continued to film.

"Scott!"

He finally laid his camera on a countertop and pulled his cell phone out. "No signal."

"Robin, look through my duffel bag!" Thomas pointed to the hallway.

She stood motionless for a moment. "For what?" she finally asked.

"The emergency phone Alex gave us!" he exclaimed. "Danny, Danny," Thomas shook her repeatedly, "Stay awake!" He tried to pick her up but was unsuccessful. Her body flopped out of his arms; she began to lose consciousness.

A loud crash resonated around the room as a metal tray full of instruments slammed to the floor. The group jumped altogether. "Robin, the phone!" Thomas broke the silence.

Robin handed it over with a blank look on her face, "What was that?"

"Scott," Thomas pulled him from his trance, "Check it out would you?"

He grabbed his camera back and ventured over to where the sound reverberated from. A large, black figure blocked out the light from the hallway for a moment. Scott drew back, "What the hell?" He stepped through the doorway against his best judgment, "Hello? Is someone there?"

"No, don't!" Robin warned him.

Scott peered over his shoulder, Thomas tended to Danielle on the ground and Robin stared back at Thomas with a blank look. Scott turned around and decided not to follow the shadowy figure. He lay his beloved camera down once again and headed over to Danielle. He bent down and grabbed her hand, "Danny, Danny," he whispered, "don't let go."

"I'm going to try this phone," Thomas said, "Keep her awake." He walked to the door where the figure vanished.

Thomas paced up and down the hallway and begged for help. "Hello, can you hear me?"

The voice on the other side was very faint and static clogged the line, "Hell…Who is…What do…Want?

"This is Thomas Flynn at the Elizabeth Anne Institute. Alex Kinkaid sent us here for a uh…a special assignment."

"What's your…ution?" the jumbled voice asked.

"Excuse me? Um, a team member is bleeding, she needs medical assistance. There were needles sticking out of her arms when we found her."

"What's…mptoms?"

"Blood from her eyes, she was convulsing. Does it matter? Please, just help us!"

"Okay, we just needed confirmation from Alex, we're on our way. Keep her conscious."

Derrick Smith

Chapter 7

FINALLY FOUND SOMETHING

Danielle stirred in her linen clad cot. She tried to open her eyes, but severe pain shot up and down her spine. She was finally able to force her eyes open but could not make out anything but blurry spots. The pain grew so immense, so she closed her eyes once again. After a few minutes passed, she tried to view her surroundings once again. This time, color shone through the blurred spots, a lot of white and a lengthy puke green. Danielle opened her mouth, "Heeee!" she squeaked. She tried once more, "Plll!" She could make nothing more than sounds. *What's wrong with me?* she thought. Unable to speak, she tried to get someone's attention, so Danielle began to shake. Her body shook the small cot she laid on so rapidly, it nearly tipped over.

A figure rushed into the room; he was draped in green from head to toe with a similar colored face mask. "Hold still now," the figure commanded.

Danielle's vision slowly came back to her. The figure in front of her wore a small pair of glasses and had a long, curled mustache. "Dooo?" she attempted to ask.

"Just lay still," the man exclaimed. He pulled out a long, colossal syringe.

"Nnnn!" Danielle tried to scream. She made her body shake yet again.

The doctor put the syringe on a tiny, metal table next to the makeshift bed. "Hold her down!"

"Heee mmm!" Danielle shrieked.

A tall man stepped forward out of the dark shadows, "Doctor, what's wrong with her?" He was dressed in a blue Armani suit, his face still shrouded in shadows. He peered over Danielle, "Can't she talk?"

The doctor glanced down toward Danielle. He grabbed the syringe from the table. He squirted it a few times. The warm liquid fell to the cot and Danielle began to shake.

"Grab her!" the doctor shouted.

"Nnnn…Plll!" tears rolled down Danielle's cheeks.

The suited man held her down as the doctor jammed the needle into her side. "Keep her still. This won't take long," the doctor explained.

Danielle writhed in pain as the needle drew out of her abdominal area. "Pllee!" her voice, as well as her consciousness faded, slowly, slowly.

"How could this happen?" Thomas questioned the sole doctor on call. "No kid or bum had access to medical supplies."

Aaron sat on the floor in the hallway next to Thomas, his head lay in his hands. "It's my fault. If I were only there to protect her, I…I…"

"I'm not all that –" the doctor was interrupted.

"No!" a booming voice sounded from behind the doctor, hidden in the few shadows that still remained in the building.

Thomas squinted into the darkness, "Alex?"

"How you doing' Tommy boy?" Alex walked out of the darkness. "I'm guessing not well," he chuckled.

Thomas glared at him, "How can you laugh at a time like this?"

"Because this is our lives, this is going to play into our favor, this is going to make our movie better," Alex continued to snicker.

"What?" Aaron looked up, "That's wrong!"

Alex simply disregarded Aaron's pathetic plea to save his companion. "To answer your initial question, Tommy," he sighed, "No. No one could have gotten in here without us knowing. We have cameras everywhere which are constantly monitored, deadbolts on every door, as well as padlocks."

"So what –" Aaron was interrupted.

"Are you sure she didn't…" Alex trailed off in mid-sentence.

Aaron stood and stepped toward Alex, "What? Did it herself? Shot up because of her old drug habits?" He shoved Alex hard. He flew back into the wall. "No! You're wrong!" Aaron shouted.

"Aaron! Stop!" Thomas shouted, "Not again!" Thomas grabbed him, "Control yourself!"

He calmed himself down, "I'm sorry, I…I should just go." Aaron lowered his head and made his way down the hall but looked back, "It wasn't her." He continued his course down the corridor.

"You know," Thomas looked back at Alex, "she was strapped down."

"And she did have an addiction," Alex shot back.

Thomas went on the defensive, "You tell me how. Please, Alex, explain. She unstrapped herself, shot up, and then strapped herself back down leaving the needles in her arms in what? Two minutes? Oh, right, that makes perfect sense."

The doctor interjects, "Excuse gentlemen, I need to take some blood samples. She may not have much time."

"Can't we just take her to the hospital?" Thomas asked.

Alex cackled, "Absolutely not! No one leaves; it would attract way too much negative publicity. I mean, especially with her background we would look like a bunch of amateurs. Everything we have spent, all our time, would have been a waste."

"But it's a life we're talking about!" Thomas argued. "Isn't that worth more than money or reputation?"

"May I?" the doctor once again asked.

Alex simply nodded as the doctor withdrew into the secluded room. "The shooting continues on schedule," Alex demanded.

"You didn't answer my question."

Alex shook his head, "No Tom, not just money. It's all our professional lives. Imagine what would happen to that girl," he paused. No comment from Thomas so he continued, "She would lose everything. Reputation…career…job…money…home…her life."

"What about Michael at least?"

"He'll be fine, the doctor explained that it was a simple chemical imbalance," Alex explained as though he made the diagnosis.

Thomas looked confused, "That's it? So just wait?"

"Yes, don't over complicate it, that's all there is to it," Alex reconfirmed his comment. "And don't continue shooting for yourself. Don't do this for me or the money. Do this for your team, your friends."

Thomas took a deep breath, "Okay, okay, we'll continue."

A grin grew under Alex's thick mustache, "I'm glad you agree." He chuckled, "Not like you actually had a choice."

Again, Thomas showed a perplexed look, "Whatever, enough mind games. I'm going to go join my team now. Please, please let me know let me know when you get the results."

"Oh, it won't take that long," Alex assured him. "He's the best doctor I know, we'll get the results tomorrow morning I'd say."

Thomas yawned, "Thank you very much Alex. Good night and I will talk to you tomorrow morning."

"Give me a call if I don't get hold of you first, "Alex explained. "Try not to, you know, get haunted or whatever tonight," he shot Thomas a quick smile then turned back to the room which housed Danielle.

Thomas made his way down the hallway to meet with the rest of his crew for some desperately needed sleep.

The crew sat around the kitchen table as each member tried to lay the horrid picture of Danielle to rest. By this time, Michael was released from his restraints and seemed to have returned to himself. Carrie sat next to him and held his hand tight, both in silence.

"Really guys don't worry," Thomas reassured them all. "The doctor told us that Danielle will be fine. Whatever he injected into her, well, she reacted well to it."

Aaron made his way to his feet from the bed he rested on, "It's my fault. If I wouldn't have reacted how I did, I could have been there…" His tired body led him to his bed, "I'm sorry Robin, Scott, everyone. I truly am." He tried to hold back the tears which began to emerge.

"Really Aaron, it's okay," Robin made her way over to him. "It's really not your fault. This place got the worst of you, that's all."

Scott smirked, "Yeah, I don't –"

Thomas shot him a nasty look, "Don't!"

"What?" Scott chuckled under his breath, "I was going to say…it's not his fault."

"Sure you were," Thomas sarcastically remarked.

Robin held Aaron's hand, "Get some rest, I know you need it." She gave him a warm smile, "She'll be fine, I promise." With that, Aaron was out like a light once he rested his head on his pillow. "Keep it down guys," Robin whispered, "He's out already."

"Yes mother," Scott whispered. "I'm beat anyway; I'm going to head to sleep in my little cot."

Thomas and Robin made their way to the door as Scott got ready for bed.

"I think we're actually going to hit the hay too," Carrie announced softly. Michael still kept quiet as a mouse.

"Good night guys," Thomas said. "We'll see you in the morning for some more fun," his sarcastic tone did not sit well.

Scott mumbled, "Right. Go to hell, oh wait, we're already there."

Robin shoved the door open, "Come on Tommy, we should discuss tomorrow."

The crew dispersed to their separate rooms, aside from Danielle who was contained in a closely monitored, new quarantine room down the hall, which was transformed from one of the old patients' rooms. Thomas and Robin strolled leisurely down the still bright hall.

"We're not actually going to talk about tomorrow," Thomas forced a smile, "Are we?"

Robin flashed him a quick smirk, "Well I actually wanted to find out what really happened tonight." She pulled a flashlight out of her bag, "And I figured we could help investigate it to help with the process."

"Now I remember why I fell for you," Thomas winked.

Robin could do nothing less than smile while her cheeks flushed once more, "Yeah, remember when we tried that? It ended in a…" she tried to muster up the right word, "Well, it didn't end well."

"Yeah, yeah, that's too bad though. Anyway, just out of curiosity, do you think she did it to herself?" Thomas tried to get back on point.

Taken back by the quick turnaround, it took a moment for Robin to reply, "Goodness no," she seemed almost offended. "I think some drugged up junkie made his way in, she saw him, he panicked, and stabbed her, leaving his drugs behind when she screamed."

"Why would the junkie waste his…stuff on her?"

"Like I said," she explained, "he panicked. Maybe he thought it would make her forget about him or keep her quiet. I don't know what those kinds of people think, they barely have any brain cells left anyway."

Thomas held up the camera, "Interesting, to each their own, opinion that is."

Robin smiled, "You know Tommy, I'm really glad you guys hired me. It's really good to see you again."

"Same here," Thomas grinned back, "It's been what? Three years?"

She held her hand out, "More, what do you think anyway? You know, getting back on topic."

Thomas handed over the camera, "You really want to know what I think?"

She nodded and clicked a button on the device.

"I believe, after years of experience and attempts of contacting the deceased, that we finally found something," Thomas paused and glanced over his shoulder. "I think that both the murderous doctors and innocent patients still roam these halls. It is my strong belief that the laboratory we were in was where many patients met their brutal demise. When Danielle was strapped to the chair, we awoke something that should no longer be here. Whatever we awoke, it felt like a fearful and helpless patient. At the time, that's exactly what Danielle appeared as by the paranormal presence."

Robin's eyes grew wide with fear as goosebumps crawled down her arms.

He continued, "I wish things went differently and we didn't make contact, but I really do not think we have a choice here. There is so much pain and despair trapped in this building. So many lives were lost, and we're stuck between those poor lost souls and the next world." Thomas stared directly into the camera, "To tell you the truth, I don't think we have any way of stopping these forces. We just need to ride the bullet and get the hell out of here as soon as humanly possible."

"Wow," Robin's mouth dropped. "Okay, now I feel scared, and for some reason cold. Can we go back now?" she asked with a pair of puppy dog eyes.

Thomas smiled, "I am that good aren't I?"

"What? You made that up?"

"Oh no, no," he assured her. "I was being completely serious, I just think this place gets to some people more than others and I was trying to bring that fear out with that speech." Thomas tossed his arm around her and pulled her close, "Let's get some shut eye huh?"

The two ventured back to their hall to join the rest in slumber for what was left of the diminished night.

Eerie noises echoed throughout the asylum; doors slammed, window panes creaked, what sounded like voices reverberated in every corner of the peculiar structure. The chaotic noises ensued the entire night but the whole crew was able to slumber through the hours of darkness. All members, except one.

Michael tossed and turned in his cot, which rested directly next to Carrie's, in their tiny room. The events from the night continually played back in his mind, and he eventually grew paranoid. He frequently woke in a cold sweat and finally decided to call it quits. With Carrie passed out for the night, Michael had no one to rationalize his incoherent thoughts. He rose from his cot and began to pack his large suitcase.

While he packed, Michael began to think about Danielle and what he heard happened. *This place is pure evil*, he thought. His actions grew faster, sloppier; he needed to leave. He began to hallucinate; dark shadows reached out of the darkness, it reached for him and grabbed, even though there was no darkness in the room. *Oh God, what is going on? I need to get the hell out of here!* He once again thought to himself.

He made his way out the door; the darkness began to consume him for a second time. Before he pushed his way through the door, Michael looked back to Carrie; *Should I tell her?* He grabbed a pen and paper on the table, *I can't tell her, she won't let me leave*, he contemplated. He began to scribble on the piece of paper a goodbye note to Carrie: Take care, good luck, and thank so much for everything you did for me. I appreciate it more than you'll ever know. See you soon. Mikey.

Michael left the note on the nightstand beside their bed, then turned to the door and readied himself for his exit. He reached for his cell phone and began to dial his brother's number. "Damn," he murmured to himself. "No signal." *What'd you expect?* Michael inquired to himself. He let a slight smirk grow upon his face.

He turned a corner after a few steps outside of their modified sleeping quarters. Michael did not have a clue where to go or even where he was, so he started to walk into the darkness which only he could see. He caught a dark silhouette in his peripheral vision as it circled around him. *Another hallucination*, he contemplated.

A voice muttered in the distance, "Mike…Mike; help me."

"Danielle?" Michael asked, "Is that you?"

The figure showed itself and again Michael thought his eyes or mind was playing tricks on him. It seemingly skipped every other step, as though it were a VHS tape and began to skip frames.

"No way," Michael whispered and wiped his eyes. He could make out a woman's figure, long, brown hair, white nightgown, and a voluptuous build. "Danielle?" he began to shout now.

The figure apparently led him down the hall, around corners, all around the asylum, and finally left him at the chapel doors which hung wide open.

"Help me Mikey!" The voice grew stronger now, more violent, almost demanding. It resonated from the altar.

Michael stepped into the aged church, "Danielle?" he asked again. He noticed the podium was knocked over; there was a body underneath it! "Robin," he shook his head and thought it was a prop of hers. He walked to it and leaned over, "Danielle! No! Can you hear me?" He grabbed her hand.

Danielle's limbs were limp and she could barely talk but was able to mutter a few words, "Help…me. It hurts so…bad."

Michael panicked, "Oh God, I've got to get you out of here!" He began to lift the podium. He witnessed blood pour out from her midsection, "Oh!"

"Wh…what's wrong?" Danielle was able to mumble.

Her bowels set in a pile next to her nearly paralyzed body. There was a large gash in her left side, most likely slit open from the corner of the bulky, heavy, pedestal. The slash, however, looked to be very perfect, a straight line from breast to hip, very neat. "Who did this?" he asked Danielle; he didn't expect to get an answer.

Tears strolled down her cheeks, "Aaron? Is that you?" She became delirious, "I'm so cold."

"It's Michael," he told her. "I'll go get Aaron, you'll be fine. We'll get help." He began to get up when Danielle clutched his arm. Suddenly her face twitched and mutated into Robin. Her curly, dirty blonde hair was tainted with thick blood stains.

"Don't go; I don't want to die alone!"

"I won't let you, Robin," his arm began to swell. "Please let go…"

Robin's face winced and twisted violently and once again contorted into another: Carrie.

"Oh God," he muttered. "Carrie, what happened?"

"Help me, please." She squeezed his arm tighter; blood began to drip down his arm from the grip of her fingernails.

Michael held his head, "What the hell?" He murmured as he tried to pull away. "Please let go, I'll get help!"

"No," she screamed. Her voice deepened and sounded almost evil. She twitched once again, she shook sadistically. Michael stepped back as the new face that was morphed into was his own. Blood poured from his dark eye sockets. Gashes opened on his cheeks, blood spilled onto the floor.

Michael tried once more to pull away from the figure in distress which now took the form of his own face. "I…I…" he was stunned. He had no idea what to do. Michael tried to yank his arm away from the figure. "No!"

"You are not leaving!"

"I need to get –" pain shot from his neck, all the way down his spine. He couldn't move. His body collapsed in a heap. The darkness consumed him once more. He tried to look around and reached toward Danielle but was paralyzed. The pain overwhelmed him, his lips reading, *Help*. From the darkness within Michael's mind, a freezing, cadaverous hand reached out and grabbed him; all grew dark.

Dawn finally broke on the Elizabeth Anne Asylum, even though the sun never shone through the gray sky. Every crew member visited Danielle once they awoke from their short night of slumber. After which, they crowded around the kitchen table. Carrie was the last to awaken.

"Mike," Carrie rolled over, "I thought I asked you to…" She trailed off once she realized Michael was gone.

She ventured past a nightstand with a small pile of ashes strewn across it, out into the kitchen to meet everyone at the table. Everyone munched on some sort of cereal drenched in milk. "Anyone see Mike this morning?" Carrie asked amidst a yawn.

Each investigator looked at one another until Thomas broke the silence, "We all thought he was with you."

"That's odd," Carrie checked her cell phone, "No signal."

Scott snickered, "Is that a surprise?" He glanced around the room quickly, "I don't think anyone has one."

Carrie looked to Thomas for advice, "What do we do?"

"Nothing, "Robin broke in, "We can't leave or do anything really."

Thomas started toward the ground, "She's right," he grunted. "Not only are we on a tight schedule, but Alex already explained that we couldn't leave for any reason." Thomas grabbed her hand, "We'll keep our eyes open, don't worry." He and Robin gave her a comforting smile.

"He's probably the only smart one among us," Scott remarked. "If I didn't need the money, I'd be right behind him."

Aaron agreed, "I'm sure he's fine, Scott's right. Especially what happened last night…and that was only the first."

"I'm worried though," Carrie sighed. "I guess there's nothing we can do anyway. He's better off away from here anyway." Silence fell about the room. "How's Danielle?"

"You're allowed to check on her you know," Scott notified her, slightly irritated. "We all did."

Carrie looked stunned, "Oh, I didn't think we could. I thought it was some sort of clean room or something."

"Nah, just an isolation room," Thomas explained. "To make sure nothing else happened and she could be monitored."

"She's doing fine though," Robin clarified, "Her arms are now a little bruised. It's probably from struggling with her restraints mixed with…well, whatever was injected in her."

Carrie stood from her seat, "I'll pop in and check on her. I'll be right back." She made for the door.

"I should give Alex a call to see if they got any results yet," Thomas explained to the group and followed Carrie out the door. "We'll all meet back at the lab where we left off last night," he gazed at his watch, "let's say a half hour?"

"You mean where Danielle was…" Aaron could not even finish his sentence.

"Yes," Robin stuck behind the decision. "We need to pick up the story right where we left off."

Thomas turned toward the door, "No question, we film in a half an hour."

The rest of the crew finished their breakfast in silence, still a little dissatisfied with the decision, changed their dingy clothes, and began to get ready for their first full day of filming.

"No! Now I have to go. Unlike some people, I am very busy."

'Click.' The phone went dead.

"Oh, thank you so much Alex. I really appreciate your time…asshole," Thomas spoke into the emergency phone. *Well, that helped oh so much*, he thought.

A loud thunderclap broke his train of thought. Rain began to pour down outside the asylum; the drops slammed off the cracked brick and made a loud 'crash' resonance.

"Perfect setting," Thomas muttered. *Back to the story*, he supposed. *Michael is straight up missing but can be replaced. Danielle is now restrained to her bed, and she was going to be a big part.*

He stopped in his tracks as the lights began to flicker violently. "Shit!" he hurried his pace to meet the crew. *There's no chance in hell I'm getting stuck in this building in the dark*, he thought.

The crew gathered in front of the aged laboratory door, where Danielle had been maliciously attacked, and awaited Thomas's arrival. The door seemed to swing open on its own but the brisk morning breeze, which somehow found its way into the old asylum, most likely had something to do with the eerie movement. The lights flickered abundantly while the air grew even colder.

"Is this right?" Aaron asked. "I mean, it doesn't feel right after what happened, you know?"

None of the crew had an answer and seemed to decide to ignore the question as a whole. "Where is he?" Robin asked, irritated. "The lights are about to go out."

"He'll be here," Scott assured them. "Don't worry, you all stress yourselves out. Just relax."

Sure enough, no more than five minutes later, Thomas shuffled down the hallway to rejoin the team. "Dear God, this place is really starting to freak me out," Thomas announced, seemingly out of breath, now hunched over.

Robin placed her arm on his arched back, "Calm down, take some breaths. Are you okay? What are you running for?"

"The lights…about to…" Thomas could barely speak, "go out."

Scott chuckled, "As we've noticed. "Anyway, do you remember anyone leaving this door open?"

Carrie nudged the door, "And do you have some sort of story worked out for this thing?"

"Come on guys," Robin interjected, "give him a break."

Thomas smiled and straightened himself back up, "Thanks Rob." He took another deep breath, "Okay, to answer your questions; yes, I have a story, and there's a lot of wind in this place. The door must have swung open with it."

Scott slung his backpack on his back and pushed open the door, "Good enough for me. Shall we?"

"Don't we need to kind of know the story first?" Carrie stammered.

Thomas shook his head and held open the door, "Nah, not really. Just go with it."

The crew filed one by one into the laboratory where Danielle had been brutally assaulted less than 24 hours before.

"Okay," Thomas motioned over to Carrie, "I need you to sort of mimic Danny and sit in that chair. And Scott, just keep your focus on me. I've got a story worked up."

Robin and Aaron stood right inside the door, "What do you want us to do?" Aaron asked.

"Uh…" Thomas took a second to think. "Just poke around a little bit I guess. Take your camera and follow Robin around to some of her prop areas. Maybe back to the morgue?"

Aaron and Robin glanced at one another until Robin finally shrugged her shoulders, "Okay Tommy, works for me. I've got some stuff set up in the morgue."

"Sounds good to me," Thomas flashed her a smile through his five o'clock shadow, "Let's get to work!"

Carrie sat in the chair and Thomas strapped her down. Scott checked for good camera angles. Aaron and Robin ventured into the secret passage from the laboratory to the morgue.

The brick encrusted hallway was dark, damp, and reeked of rotting flesh. Spider webs enveloped the water damaged ceiling. Bricks were falling out of the wall, some smashed on the floor, some missing completely.

"Man, this passageway must have been very secret," Robin contemplated. "It looks as if someone just dug it out then reinforced it with brick."

Aaron walked alongside her in silence. He stepped on a brick and faltered back, "Shit!" He caught himself against the wall.

Robin giggled silently, "Well at least –"

A large pendulum ax swung from the ceiling. Aaron noticed it with his peripheral vision and grabbed hold of Robin as they both slammed to the concrete floor. "Are you okay?" Aaron stammered.

"I'm fine," she smirked.

Aaron sat up, "You think that's funny?"

She began to giggle, "A little, yeah."

"We could have been killed! How can you think that's funny?" he demanded.

"Well," Robin stood. The pendulum lay dormant in front of her. She reached out with her hand and ran her fingers along the blade. Blood poured from her wrist as she crashed to the floor. The blood covered Aaron and splashed to the floor in a growing puddle.

"Oh God! No!" he yelled out. "No! Robin!"

"What is it?" she shook him. He snapped back to attention. "Were you daydreaming?"

"Oh, uh," Aaron stood to join her. "I guess so, yeah."

"Anyway," Robin continued. She ran her hand along the blade, "It's a hard rubber; and one of my favorite props."

"Got any more of them in here," he chuckled, trying to play off fear in a joking manner. "You know, just so I don't tackle you anymore." He winked as a smile grew across his face.

"Well…" she began. "I have stuff scattered all throughout this place. Some of them won't even set off while we're here. But I can't tell anyone or else they won't have any effect on the camera. I mean, you trying to save me; now that was a good reaction. I just hope they caught that on some hidden camera somewhere." She shared his smile.

They continued through the corridor into the oversized and seemingly unnecessary morgue. Both Robin and Aaron scoured the morgue for any possible shots or ideas for the story. Aaron moved hesitantly around the bitter room, apparently afraid that Robin's horror props would pop up and scare the be-Jesus out of him.

"You good Scott?" Thomas asked briskly after he strapped Carrie in.

Scott moved in a few different positions before he answered him, "I think so, yeah."

"Carrie?" Thomas grabbed her hand, "what about you?"

She swallowed hard, "I…think so."

"There's nothing to worry about," Thomas assured her, "We'll be right here with you."

Scott grew impatient, "It's getting really cold in here; can we get this going?"

Carrie agreed, "Good idea, the lights are starting to get worse too."

"Okay, okay, let's go." Thomas pointed to the camera.

Scott held his fingers up, "Three…two…one." The camera's red lights blinked on, and Scott signaled to Thomas.

"Back in the late 1800's, the Elizabeth Anne Mental Hospital was filled to the brim with more than 1,500 patients and only about 200 employees. This led to doctors, especially the superintendent and chief of medicine, Doctor Joseph D. Stroyne, to attempt very risky and somewhat barbaric treatments on the overabundant patients and limited resources. They performed simple treatments, such as hydrotherapy and the ever-common solitude."

"Hydrotherapy was when patients were submerged in tubs for hours on end, in hot or cold water, in order to shut out all other sensations. The doctors also locked patients up in seclusion rooms; strapped them in straight jackets, handcuffs, or crude leg cuffs, just simply to get them out of their hair." Thomas laughed, "And these were the rational, ethical treatments of the time."

"Now where we stand, this…this is the laboratory. To some patients, this was hell. To others, more than 1,300 patients, this room was the last thing they ever saw. Most perished from the very hands of Doctor Stroyne, himself. His favor types of treatment, or torture, included his very own version of the frontal lobotomy, which, his nurses said, was used a little excessively. The procedure was fatal for eight out of every ten patients. Stroyne also experimented with the newly developed drug, Thorazine; a dramatic approach to heal the mentally ill. The most common side effect, which almost always led to death, was severe seizures and bleeding through the eyes. The legal version of this drug was not released until 1950, over 60 years later."

Thomas took a deep breath, "No matter what outcome, even if the patient did show vast improvement, the doctor would not accept it. For his thought was that mental illness cannot be cured no matter what the disease. Many of Stroyne's failed, and possibly successful experiments, can be seen in the medical monstrosity museum in Philadelphia, the Mutter Museum."

"So," Thomas posed the question to the audience, "if the doctor did not think patients with mental illnesses could be cured; why experiment? Why try at all?" The lights flickered violently, doors slammed but there was no wind, and the crew could see their breath in the now cold ambiance which filled the room. "Was what happened to Danielle a slight example of what happened to the many innocent patients who perished in this very room?"

Carrie began to tremble in her constraints, "Please, guys, let me out!"

Thomas continued but raised his voice, "We'll do a little experiment and see what happened to Danielle by strapping our very own crew member, Carrie, into the exact same chair, in the exact same position. Will Doctor Stroyne perform the same experiments on her? Doctor…where are you? Show yourself!"

A loud shriek echoed from the connected morgue; it was Robin.

"Stay with her," Thomas commanded Scott. He rushed to the barely visible entrance.

"Please Scott, help me!" Carrie pleaded.

"Just wait," Scott demanded and pointed the camera toward the morgue's entrance. "Tom, is everything okay?"

Thomas continued to the morgue; a pale look grew upon his face.

Scott could only make out mumbles a few cuss words until Thomas shouted, "Scott! You should get in here…and keep rolling!"

"Wait! Please, help me!" Carrie bellowed.

Scott ignored her and followed Thomas through the tiny, undeveloped hallway. It opened up into a huge, agape, catacomb which housed hundreds upon hundreds of crypts; some still held the remains of tortured patients at the hands of Doctor Stroyne. He finally noticed what had disturbed Aaron, Robin, and Thomas. The concrete floor was soaked with what looked like large puddles and streaks of blood. Scratches could be seen, as if someone was dragged along the surface, dead fingernails wedged amidst the vein-like blood streaks.

Thomas looked at Robin, "That's amazing. How'd you do this?" He was amazed and extremely impressed; until he saw her face, "Robin, you did this right?"

Her cheeks grew pale, as if she had seen a ghost. Her hands shivered, as if a sudden burst of cold air stung her, "I...no."

"Turn that off!" Thomas again demanded Scott. He looked back to Robin, "This is very realistic; almost too realistic. Who could have pulled this off?"

She simply shook her head.

Scott pointed across the room, past the blood streaks, to a doorway lined with frosted, plastic flaps, "Um, does anyone know what the hell that is?"

"The autopsy room..." Thomas trailed off in astonishment.

"Help!!!" Carrie screamed from her position in the chair back in the laboratory. "Please, someone!"

Thomas glanced toward Robin, "Go get Carrie. We'll be here."

Robin just shook her head once more, "No, I'm already scared out of my mind." She looked back to Thomas, "You get her."

"Fine," Thomas seemed stunned, "No big deal." He turned toward the undeveloped hallway, which led back to the lab. "I'll be right —" he was cut off as a shadowy figure approached from the other side of the hall. "Gu...gu...guys," he beckoned for help. "Guys!" Thomas stumbled to the ground. On his hands and knees, he attempted to reach the group. The shadowy figure grew larger, then suddenly…"Come on Carrie! You scared the living shit out of me!"

Carrie pulled herself out of the restraints and followed the rest of the crew, "You deserve a lot worse, you son of a bitch." She waited for him to regain his composure, "Why did you leave me back there to be attacked?"

A confused look cultivated over Thomas's pale face, "Wait…what? I thought you were restrained to the chair."

Carrie offered her hand, "You scared the piss out of me, so I decided to return the favor." She smiled, "But can you please just not do that again? I don't like this place one bit."

"You and everyone else. Don't worry," Thomas made his way to his feet with the help of Carrie. "We're going to finish this as fast as possible." He gave her a warm smile, "Now let's go. They're waiting for us in the autopsy room."

Carrie followed in Thomas's footsteps, "Wait, what? Why would they need an autopsy room here?"

"I guess we're about to find that out." The two finally entered the large, eerie, corpse-filled mausoleum to meet the rest of the party.

Derrick Smith

Chapter 8

WELCOME

The autopsy room smelled of rotted flesh and formaldehyde. It was cold; a mist built up on the surface of the floor and grew nearly a foot above it. The room was empty, not a trace of a surgical instrument, old examination tables, or even the blood trail that had led the group there in the first place.

"How does a blood trail just end?" Scott questioned, obviously anxious to film something phenomenal. "Well, that was a waste of suspense!"

Thomas looked around, seemingly disappointed, "Now hold on just a second. You all can tell this 'mad doctor' was absolutely insane as well as —"

"Extremely fucked in the head," Aaron proclaimed. Scott agreed while he continued to search for something, anything.

"Not exactly the word I was looking for, but you're not wrong," Thomas continued. "This mad man was a genius. I mean, after all he *was* able to hide nearly all of the experiments and murderous activity until the place was taken over and Stroyne disappeared."

Robin looked back, outside of the frigid tomb, "Tom, I don't know how much longer I can stay in here." Her cheeks flushed as she began to gag.

"Ugh, she's right," Aaron agreed. "It reeks of…death."

Thomas seemed disgusted, "Now hold on a second. Look around for anything odd, or out of place."

"What?" Scott laughed, "Like a trap door?"

Thomas smiled, "Exactly."

"Um, I think I'll pass on the childish games there Tommy," Scott shot back arrogantly. "Besides," he glanced over to Robin, "she's about to blow chunks."

Robin held her stomach, "I really have to get out." She couldn't take it anymore and began to walk back to the plastic flaps.

Scott ran over to her and grabbed her arm, "Come on let's –" he stopped as the two crashed to the floor. "What the hell?" Scott looked around as the two lay in the fog.

A grinding noise began as the floor vibrated. "What's going on?" Aaron shouted over the buzzing and creaking.

"I don't know!" yelled Thomas. The creaking turned into moaning, then humming, "It sounds like the grinding of cranks of some sort!"

Suddenly, the middle of the autopsy room split apart, revealing a single, metal examination table. It rose slowly through the concrete floor; the crew was in shock.

"Well, I guess we found the secret lever!" Scott shouted.

"Robin, are you okay?" Aaron bellowed.

She looked around as she gained her footing, "Yeah, I think I'm…" Robin trailed off as she felt something warm and sticky on her hands, "Am I bleeding?"

Thomas worked his way around the now fully erect table, "I don't think so." The loud crunching noise began to slow down and eventually stop. "Thank God for that!"

"Why is there blood on my hands?" Robin began to panic. She looked to the floor; there were puddles of blood which emerged along with the table. "Um, Tom…" she pointed to the table.

Aaron already stood beside it, in a trance, he just stared. Something sat on the table, a black cloth covered it. "Is this a joke? A prop? Please God, say it is." He ran his fingers over his buzzed head, and then reached his hand down to the table, "Should I?"

"No…It wasn't," Robin trailed off in disbelief.

The rest of the crew gathered around the crude slab, likely used to examine the remains of lost patients. "No, wait!" Scott beckoned, "Let me grab my camera."

"This isn't the time Scott," Thomas shot him a disdainful look. "Robin just said she didn't do this."

"Yes it is. This is why we're here after all isn't it?" Scott clicked the camera on and a small, red button flashed on. A small red light flashed on, "This shit is real, and this is going to make us rich," a smirk showed on his face.

Thomas reached up to the camera, "I'm serious, put it down!"

Scott looked around for some support from his peers; it never came. "Alright, alright; chill out."

"Go ahead," Thomas nodded to Aaron, "Lift it."

He reached down once more to the cloth, "It's sticky." He pulled his hand back up, "It's blood."

Thomas rubbed the cloth, pulled up some of the sticky substance. He smelled it, then pulled away, "Oh...let's get this over with. Pull it off!"

Once more, Aaron grabbed hold of the blood-soaked sheet. This time however, he heaved it upward. The crew gasped as they witnessed the gruesome terror which lay beneath. Blood poured off the table like a waterfall, the body was undistinguishable. The face was torn completely off, the abdomen split open in the shape of an 'X,' both legs bent the wrong way and revealed whitish gray bone, and the arms were on backwards! They seemed to have been cut off cleanly and stitched back on the opposite side they came from.

Robin turned away and spewed, "I'm done; this is bullshit. I want out." She stomped through the flaps, back out into the oversized morgue.

The rest of the crew stood around in shock, not a clue what to do. "Carrie," Thomas paused and swallowed hard, "is that...is that Michael?" He pointed to the blood-soaked black jeans he noticed him in the day before.

Tears emerged from Carrie's eyes as she clutched the corpse's hand. "No! Mikey, I'm so sorry. This can't be happening; this is impossible! What did he ever do to you?" She seemed to direct her anger toward the house; stomped her feet, punched the walls. "Tom, what do we do? I don't know if I can stay here after this shit."

"I...I," he had no idea, nor did anyone else. "I'll call Alex; whatever is happening is out of our control. We need to leave."

Scott peered over the group of onlookers who surrounded the remains of Michael. The red light flickered on as he began to film the gruesome scene. "Oh God, this is disgusting," his mouth agape.

"Knock it the hell off!" Thomas grabbed the camera and pulled it away from Scott. "This is not the time!" Scott backed off, like a scared puppy dog with its tail between its legs. "Now, if you all don't mind, I'm going to give Alex a call, and hopefully he'll get us out of here." He turned to exit and to get some peace and quiet, "Don't anyone go near him! Not one of you!"

Alex rushed to the asylum as soon as Thomas explained the situation to him. It only took about a half an hour to arrive.

"Should we call it off?" Thomas's voice boomed through the hall. "I mean there have already been two unexplainable incidents."

Alex took a deep breath, "Look," he grabbed Thomas's arm and pulled him to the side. "We need the money, we need the new equipment, and most importantly we need the recognition right now. If we back out now, we lose all of that."

"Yes, but is it really worth the lives? That…murder was just…disgusting and out of this world." Thomas tried to convince Alex.

Alex shook his head, "No, the team is willing to accept the risks that come with the job, they have always known what –"

"Don't you mean my team?" a shadowy figure walked out from behind Alex. "This is my old show, and we didn't have to fake it. Do you remember those days, assistant?"

"Max? What the hell? Why are you…why is he here?" Thomas stammered.

"I was approached weeks ago by Alex and his boys to act as a backup. They all knew you were going to fuck up!" Max bellowed.

Thomas was taken back and was unable to respond; his cheeks flushed, and he looked back to Alex, "So what do we do now?"

"Well first things first. The doctor gave me the results this afternoon. The tests showed traces of sulfonylurea in Danielle's blood stream. It's a drug that was used here in the early days of the hospital to thin blood before doctors bled their patients. However, in the late 50's, it was proven to block the blood flow and cause spasms in certain cases; this was the cause of the bloody tears. The traces are being depleted as we speak and should be completely passed through her system in another day or so."

A feeling of relief cultivated over Thomas, "Okay, that's good news, but what's *his* role here on out? And what are we doing about Michael?"

The lights flickered violently yet again, and cries of pain echoed down the halls. "He's going to help you all survive a few more days. And don't worry about him, we'll get that cleaned up and your crew will be able to finish their job."

"A few more days? How about until we're done?" Thomas interjected.

Alex cleared his throat, "Well, about that…"

"Yes?"

"We sold the facility to NAW Research Systems. They are going to demolish this very building over the weekend and begin construction on their state of the art research center," Alex explained.

Max stepped in, "And I figure we'll have the movie done by then and can film the demolition and toss it in at the end credits."

Alex shook his head in agreement, "Good idea, Max. Now I remember why I liked you." The two snickered.

"Okay, so let me get this right," Thomas was perturbed. "Now we're on a time frame *and* I lost control of my team?"

"No, not at all, Max is simply here to…supervise," Alex assured Thomas. "I'm going to have my boys take the body for an examination. Remember, I'm only a call away."

Thomas nodded.

Max continued to grin, "You got it."

"Now, I'll let you two alone to discuss plans." Alex turned from the two investigators and made his way down the hallway. The lights continued to flash.

Max followed Thomas back to their modernized wing of the building, both in complete silence.

Scott and Aaron were both examining the video and pictures of Michael's death, which Scott had shot earlier in the night, in their makeshift dark room. The pictures seemed slightly distorted, a little blurry and the color appeared faded, nearly black and white.

"Was there something wrong with this film?" Aaron asked Scott.

He looked very closely at some of the pictures, "No, not at all. It was all in perfect condition. I don't know what happened…"

Aaron peered over Scott's shoulder, "You get a good one?"

"Um…I…" Scott stuttered. "Look."

Aaron grabbed the picture and a magnifying glass. After a moment, the color faded from his face. "Is that…"

"I think so," Scott gulped hard.

"His guts, the intestines, they look to be…" he pointed to the pile of bloody mucus left on the table next to the sewn up incision.

Scott turned away, "Removed, then…replaced?"

Aaron looked at Scott in utter confusion. "It looks like they were removed," Scott pointed to the deep cuts in his flesh. He patted the picture where blood streaks were left on the table and explained, "Then it seems as though his insides were set on the table, then…" He trailed off. "It almost looks like they were…reinserted. But why?" Scott shook his head, his thick black hair shifted back and forth. "What's that?" He pointed to the lacerations on the abdomen.

"Is that stitching?" Aaron questioned.

"Looks like someone tried to sew him back up," Scott exclaimed.

"We got to show this to the crew. There's something really fucked up going on." Aaron made a mad dash for the door.

Scott scratched his head, still in awe from the picture. "I'll stay here; see if I can dig anything else up."

Aaron was already out the door, eager to show the new find to the group.

"Yeah, sure, go show them, I'm sure they'll be excited. I'll be here, don't worry!" Scott yelled out the door, slightly aggravated. He knelt back down to the small tub and continued his development process. Scott peered back over his shoulder, *is someone there?* He felt as though he was being watched. Then suddenly a loud crash boomed behind him. The medical tray, which held all of his film tools, collapsed in a heap of twisted metal. Scott jumped up and spun around, "Hello?" He panicked and swirled around. Scott ran for the door, but began slipping in a puddle of something wet and sticky.

Scott groaned as he rolled over, "What in the…" He was covered in blood; he tried to get up but could not. His arms felt dead and could only squirm on the cold, now dark red concrete. "Hellll!" he could barely even make a sound. His body went cold, then numb, "Please, someone…" he trailed off into the darkness, while a dark figure stood over him, a skull-like face with dead, black eyes pierced deep into his motionless body.

"How are you feeling?" Robin asked Danielle, finally released from her seclusion.

Danielle stretched, reached out with both arms, and scratched her head, "I feel better than ever actually. I was just scared to death; I really thought I was dying."

"So did we," Carrie joined the pair. "I didn't see it, but I heard your screams and knew something terrible had happened."

"I just thank God that Doctor Norstye knew what he was doing," Danielle uttered.

Robin peered over Danielle's shoulder, "Who?"

"You know, the doctor that Alex hired," Danielle seemed confused. "Wait, you don't know him?"

"Well," Carrie too looked over at Danielle.

Danielle finally spun around, "What are you guys looking at?"

Two dark silhouettes strolled down the hallway, toward the threesome. Their faces grim and impassive, the lights flickered rapidly around them as they drew closer.

"Okay, I've had enough of this shit!" Carrie yelled.

"Calm down," Robin tried to assure her with a calm tone.

"Look what happened to Danielle. Look what happened to Mike. How in the fuck am I supposed to calm down?"

Danielle still seemed confused, "What happened to Mike? Alex said something about him disappearing, but did something else happen?"

"What's with all the screaming?" the voice boomed throughout the hall, obviously derived from the two figures.

The group of women looked at each other then back down the hall, none of them sure what to do.

"Danielle?" the voice echoed, "Is that you?"

Danielle cocked her head to the side, "Tommy?"

Thomas rushed over to Danielle and wrapped his arms around her, "I can't believe you're okay. What happened was just…just…"

Danielle smiled at him, "It's okay, I know what happened was a phenomenon."

Robin looked over to Max. "Who's that?" she whispered.

"Oh, right." Thomas motioned to Max, "This is Max Angel, he –"

"Is the original," Robin interrupted. She stuck her hand out to greet him, "Nice to meet you Mr. Angel. I was – or uh, am a huge fan of your work."

"Nice to meet you. And you are?" Max asked.

Robin glanced toward Thomas whose cheeks were flushed and pretended to not pay attention to Max's appeal to the group. "I'm Robin Vogel, I guess I just missed meeting you back when it was your team."

"Well, it was never our decision to get rid of him," Thomas explained. "It was Alex and the whole –"

"You know that's bullshit!" Max argued. "It's entirely your fault, you had some deal worked out with that asshole's boss so you could make all the money and get all the fame with your fake show!"

Thomas was taken back, "No, that's just not —"

Max simply stared at him, "You knew I wouldn't let the team hire a specialist and make this fake, so you took it upon yourself to 'move on' with the show."

The two continued to stare each other down.

"Well, it's very good to see you," Danielle offered him a hug.

Max took a step back, "You were just as much to blame, Danny. Don't even get me started." The group sat in silence for what seemed like hours. "Now, if you all don't mind; I am going to do my job and actually investigate this asylum."

Thomas stepped aside, "Have fun. I hope you find something that can help with our...predicament." He grinned and turned back toward his crew.

An ear piercing shriek reverberated down the hall, "What the hell was that?" Max looked back to the three investigators.

"Oh, I have those on timers. Nothing to worry about," Robin assured him. "I also have the lights, doors creaking, and other creepy stuff paired up with the screams."

Max shook his head, "So you're their savior, huh?" He turned back and continued to walk into the hallway, smothered with flickering lights, "I didn't really think you'd be the one they'd hire in order to get rid of me...and replace Chuck."

"Who's Chuck?" Robin asked.

Thomas grabbed her arm, "Why do you like this guy so much?" he whispered.

"I'm just curious. Why's it matter anyway?" Robin grew irritated.

Max shouted, "Robin, he's a jackass! Never listen to him, or his bitches."

"Don't mind him, he's always had a chip on his shoulder," Thomas paused. "Anyway, Chuck was the other guy that was uh, let go, along with Max."

"So why isn't he here?" Carrie asked, "I mean Max is back, and you've been here."

"It's kind of impossible," Danielle butted in, "He's dead."

Carrie and Robin both looked at each other, in utter shock.

"Um, well that would have been some good information to know before I signed onto this shit, you know, a few years ago," Robin shouted in disgust.

Carrie just looked down, "Death just follows you doesn't it?"

"No, no it's nothing like that, he was..." Danielle trailed off.

"There was a grave mistake during his last show," Thomas continued. "Long story short, the house we were investigating collapsed and he was trapped inside."

Silence filled the room, "I really wish you guys would have told me this, especially you Tom," Robin told him.

"I *am* sorry Robin, but that was a memory I just didn't want to remember," Thomas grabbed a map out of his backpack. "But we do need to get back to work and finish this so no one else ends up like Michael."

Robin and Carrie seemed very hesitant about continuing their jobs after they found out about Chuck and how Max was fired. "I don't know, maybe we should just call it quits," Robin suggested.

Carrie seemed to agree, and merely nodded her head along with Robin.

"Okay, then you two can find some way out of this place," Thomas argued. "Have fun, let's go Danny."

Danielle walked to him as they prepared to finish their movie, "I don't know Tom; maybe they're right."

"Oh, you too? Wow I guess I'm on my own. That's just fucking amazing!" Thomas shouted and turned away.

The three crew members stared in amazement as Thomas followed Max's path down the hallway.

"Wait Tom," Robin bellowed, "Let's finish this!"

He turned back and smiled momentarily, "Okay then, let's get to it. I have this idea –"

"Okay, okay," Danielle stepped forward, "I'm in." She looked back at Carrie, "Coming?"

Carrie looked around, "Do I have a choice? I'm not going to be left here by myself. I guess I'm in."

Thomas grinned, "Okay," he rolled out the map to the asylum. "I think we should split up into two groups. We'll both get a hand held camera, and while we're finishing this, we'll need to find Scott and Aaron."

"Wait, where'd they go?" Danielle questioned.

"Yeah, I thought they were in their makeshift print room or whatever," Robin uttered.

Thomas grabbed a small flashlight, "Nope. I thought that too, but when Max and I walked past, the light was off, and the room was empty." He shined the light on the map.

"Great," Robin said sarcastically, "Another one bites the dust."

"Don't say that", Danielle declared. "I'm sure they just went to get more footage of that autopsy room."

Thomas pointed to the map, "Which is why we're going to continue while searching for them." He looked around, "May I continue?"

Everyone nodded in silence.

"Good, now Robin and I will start in the seclusion room and work our way back into the lab and autopsy room," he moved his finger along the map. "And you guys," Thomas motioned toward Carrie and Danielle. "You guys will start in the treatment room, right beside where we will finish."

"The faster the better, right?" Carrie asked.

Thomas shook his head, "Exactly." He stood, packed the map and light, "Well, whenever you guys are ready."

"Let's finish this," Danielle stood as well. "I just want to get out of here and this seems like the best way."

"Same here," Robin agreed. "You have the cameras?"

Thomas reached in his pack, "Right here." He handed a small, hand held camera to Danielle and Robin, "Sorry, this is all we got. The dark room was empty, so they must have taken the equipment with them."

"Works for me, let's get the hell out of here," Carrie was the last to agree.

Chapter 9

SPREAD OUT

The seclusion room was damp and very bleak. Even though the lights still flickering throughout the room, it was enveloped in the whitish-green walls; the mold and mildew had overtaken the once sparkling white padded walls.

Robin held the handheld camera up, which she was given to help the team speed up their recording process, "Okay, ready?" she asked. She blinked rapidly as she tried to make out the screen on the camera.

"Probably as ready as I'll be," Thomas flinched, "these lights are so bright."

Robin clicked the button on the top and held it in, "Can't you stop them from shimmering like this?"

He shook his head, "I tried, and I actually turned them off using that remote." He stood by the only entrance and exit in the wretched room. "These lights, this place, all have a mind of their own." Thomas held his hand up; then waved her on, "Okay, let's go."

The red light flashed on, Robin pointed toward him after she counted down from three.

"This is the mad doctor's last resort before sending his patients to their doom in his laboratory." He allowed Robin to circle around him, "Patients would be brought here after anything they did wrong. The nurses were told to treat the mentally ill as children, and the doctor meant it. Doctor Stroyne informed his assistant doctors and nurses to strap the patients down to a single chair after any slight mishap, anything from tripping down the hall to speaking like any regular person, seemingly healed from their psychotic state. He found a way to punish them all, no matter what the patient did; good or bad."

Thomas pointed to the center of the room, "This is where they were strapped down." There were four holes, spaced equally apart, seemingly used to hold the chair to the concrete. "The patients were simply to be left alone in this small, three foot by five-foot closet for hours on end, but this was not the case at all. The mad doctor had his mindless nurses drain their blood, much like doctors in medieval times. Now, he didn't think this would cure them, simply drain them of all fluids and take away all ambition of being 'normal' or any intelligent thoughts." Robin cringed behind the camera; her mouth hung wide open.

"Usually after this process, he would peel their face off, using absolutely no anesthesia. He said he thought the pain would wake them up from their stupor, but everyone who knew Stroyne knew that he only wanted them to feel pain and suffering." With this statement Thomas motioned to his face as if he peeled it back. "He then would sew another victim's face on to attempt to give them a new identity. During this process, he would shave their head and strip them of all clothing but their undergarments. This was done because he knew these patients would end up in his laboratory and wanted to speed up his process before the building was shut down and his program terminated. But before he finished them in the same old ways, Stroyne would release the patients to the other, less…insane mental patients." He paused and shook his head.

"This was considered by his nurses as their 'final walk.' This was when the recently operated on patients would take the slow stroll back to the dining areas and rooms where the more stable patients resided. The outcome was never good," Thomas pushed open the seclusion room door and motioned Robin out, "this was what patients would see as they were guided by their nurses."

Robin stepped out into the hall, as she turned the corner out of the door, a shadow flashed across the hall. She gasped and turned to Thomas. "What the hell was that?"

Thomas stared off into the distance. "What was what?" He took a step past her.

"There was something, a figure moved across over there," Robin pointed down the hall.

"Let's check it out," Thomas moved toward the old security area where Robin noticed some movement. "Over he-"

A large body moved out of the shadows, into the dark room where Scott and Aaron were last known to be. The figure blended in with the flashing lights and disappeared once again, this time into the dark room.

Thomas was left speechless as he waved to Robin. He pushed the door open very cautiously, afraid of what he would find.

Danielle and Carrie headed in the opposite direction of Robin and Thomas; they were headed toward the violent wing's dining room where Doctor Stroyne would continue to torment his patients. Every so often, screams would echo down the hallway and eventually lose all scare effect on the pair.

"Why doesn't she turn her damn props and sound effects off?" Carrie protested, "I mean isn't this all real enough?"

Danielle glanced over, "Do you always complain this much? I mean I took your spot and look what happened." Silence. "Just be thankful you didn't have to go through what I did. Can we just finish this please?"

Carrie continued her pace, "Okay, I'm sorry. I just want to get out of here."

The dining room was lined with what looked like old, rotted, barber chairs, complete with arm, foot, and neck straps.

"What the hell? I thought this was supposed to be some elegant dining room for the mentally ill," Carrie glared back at Danielle.

She simply shook her head, "This guy tortured these poor souls all the time, no matter what they were doing." She held the small camera up to capture all of the grotesque footage. "Did he strap them down to feed them?"

"Didn't Tom say that the doctor would feed his patients parts of former victims?" Carrie asked, nearly gagging as she spoke.

"He basically made them into cannibals, most likely making them even crazier," Danielle mumbled. "This is disgusting."

"Can we go now?" Carrie asked. "We got his footage."

Danielle looked back to her, "Yes, please lets…" she trailed off.

"What's wrong?" Carrie noticed what stole Danielle's attention. A light shined through the opening of a small door in the opposite corner of the dining room. "Doesn't that go to the outside?"

Danielle stood in a daze, "I didn't think there were any secret rooms in this place."

Carrie shook her head, "Let me see that camera." She grabbed it from Danielle's hand, "Let's see what Robin did now." She made her way slowly to the door, Carrie ventured into the dimly lit room while Danielle stood astonished in the same spot.

A large metal bed lay in the center of the undiscovered room, a figure on top of the bed. Carrie stepped closer; the camera outstretched in her hand. "Danielle, come here. Look at this," she whispered.

Danielle reluctantly made her way into the clandestine room, "What is…"

Carrie spun around, "This is –" the look of terror on Danielle's face cut her off. She turned back toward the table.

The figure on the table, seemingly a child, pale, mutilated, and stitch-enveloped, began to rise. The child turned its head in the direction of the two disturbed individuals. The lights flickered rapidly and shut off momentarily.

Carrie had fallen back onto Danielle; she knocked her to the concrete floor. Both women shuffled out of the room, they practically crawled back into the dining area.

Thomas entered the dark room and looked down after he felt something sticky on the floor, "What the…"

A cold, clammy hand reached out from the darkness and grabbed Thomas. He nearly toppled over from the initial shock. "Whoa! Watch your step there buddy."

"Get back!" Robin shouted, "Whoever you are, get away from him!"

Thomas took a step toward Robin, "Who the hell…how did you…"

The figure entered the light. "You all need to calm down and take control of your emotions."

"Max, you bastard," Thomas grimaced. "What are you doing here? We already –"

Max shined his flashlight down to the floor, "Look what you stepped in." It was a fresh puddle of blood; streak marks lead away from the puddle and to a body curled up in the fetal position.

"Scott!" Thomas shrieked. "Scott, can you hear me?" The three gathered around him and tried to help him up.

Scott knelt without a problem, "Uh fin uh prul."

"What the hell?" Robin whispered.

"What's wrong with him?" Thomas asked.

Scott tried to stand after he slurred his words once more. After he stood for only a moment he tumbled into Max's arms.

"You okay, my man?" Max asked.

Thomas noticed Max's blood-stained shirt, "Where'd that come from?"

Robin snatched the flashlight out of Max's hand. She pointed the light beam on Scott. "Oh God."

Blood seeped from his mouth, drops of blood led to a metal operation tray which sat on the opposite side of the room. Robin followed the trail with the light, everyone was in awe with what they saw; Scott's tongue lay on the tray. It looked as though it was cut cleanly out of his mouth. Pictures set beside his seemingly surgically removed tongue. They seemed as though they were taken during the sick and twisted operation.

"We've gotta get him out of here," Thomas commanded.

Max was still in disbelief, "How...what..."

The attention turned back to Scott as he flew backward against the wall and began to convulse. He went into shock after he saw his own tongue removed from his mouth.

"We need to stop the bleeding," Robin stated.

"Where's the other camera man?" Max questioned. "There were two, weren't there?"

Robin took off her sweatshirt, "Pick his head up."

Thomas fell to his knees and lifted Scott's head, "I don't know, Max. One thing at a time, we really need to help him now." He looked up to Max, "Can you –" he was gone.

"Forget him," Robin bellowed. "We need to stop the bleeding!"

Max heard screams and headed toward them. He turned the corner, passed the chapel toward the violent patient wing. The screams grew louder with every step he took. Max finally pinpointed where the cries derived; the other group of investigators, Danielle and Carrie huddled outside of the dining hall.

"What happened ladies?" Max solicited.

They both whimpered continually. "There's a girl," Danielle wept.

"She's alive, but…but shouldn't be," Carrie continued.

Max merely appeared extremely confused, "Okay, how about you just show me?"

The two women glanced at one another as if they looked for an "okay" to enter the room once more. After a brief delay, Carrie and Danielle nodded simultaneously and followed Max into the secret room hidden within the dining area.

Max made his way slowly, carefully into the unknown room. He was taken back momentarily as the ghastly child jumped up from the metal table; suddenly a smirk grew on his face. "You guys are kidding me, right?"

Both investigators still looked frightened from their first encounter.

Max walked behind the tale; he did not even pay attention to the child. He reached back and grabbed hold of a thick, black cord. With a quick jerk of his wrist, Max had stopped the dummy on the table. "It was a prop. One of Robin's no doubt."

Carrie and Danielle were relieved; they backed out into the dining room.

"Thank you, thank you," Danielle reached out to hug Max; he backed away like before.

"I don't think so," he turned back toward the hall. "One of your camera men is in trouble. We need to find him and a phone that works."

Carrie panicked, "No, not this again." She stepped back, "No, no, no."

"Calm down," Danielle grabbed her. "What do you need us to do?"

Max took a breath, "We need to find Arlin; he's supposed to have the phone."

"You mean Aaron?" Danielle questioned; her breaths increased.

"Yeah, yeah, whatever. We need to hurry though," Max demanded.

Danielle nodded, "Whatever you need."

Carrie glanced over to her in disbelief, "No hold on a second, I don't – "

"You don't have a choice," Danielle commanded, "What do you need us to do?"

"You two are to check the basement; it's larger so the two of you can cover more area. I'll check the chapel. If you find the phone, call the cops."

"But Thomas and Alex both said –" Carrie began.

Max showed no concern, "I don't give a flying fuck! If we don't get that phone, one person will die and another may follow."

Carrie looked over to Danielle, "Well, you were in such a rush…"

Danielle turned away, "Let's go."

Max grinned as he followed the two out the door.

Scott continued to squirm and scream. His mouth swelled and the bleeding prolonged.

"What do we do?" Robin whispered to Thomas.

He shook his head, "Just comfort him."

"We can't just leave him here to die. We need to get that phone."

Thomas stood, "You're right, where's Aaron?"

"I think he was here with Scott," she stammered.

"Shit, we have to find him. We can't stay here anymore, we need that damn phone," Thomas turned for the door. "Keep him awake, I'll be back."

"Wait, where are you going?" Robin asked. "I don't know if I can stay here by myself for long."

Thomas threw open the door, "The basement, that's the only place neither group would have checked."

"Okay, okay just please hurry, I'm scared as hell right now," Robin stuttered.

"You got it," Thomas bolted out the door to find the phone.

Robin held Scott's head in her arms, "Come now, you're going to be alright."

"Ihs th docha an na sku," Scott tried to speak.

Robin cradled him tighter and shook him gently, "Don't speak, it's alright."

Tears plummeted down his cheeks, "Ey di is, ple."

"I can't understand you," tears boiled up in her eyes now. "Wait," she stood and emptied out her backpack. She grabbed a copy of the map and a broken pencil, "Here, can you write?"

Scott nodded his head slightly.

Robin handed him the pencil and map, "Write if you can."

His hand trembled but he wrote the best he could; It was the doctor and the skull. "Ih wa th docha an na sku."

"Oh my God," Robin muttered. She began to panic, "Um, we uh, we need to get to the others." She bent down and wrapped her arm around Scott's neck, "Come on; let's get you out of here." Robin pulled him up, however she faltered, and fell backward onto the counter. Barely developed pictures flew off the countertop as the two collapsed on the pile of photographs. "Damnit, I'm so sorry Scott. Come on, come on; let's give it another shot."

He shook his head violently, "Gow! Jes gow, ge hel."

Robin nodded, and apparently understood, "Okay, I'll go. I will be back for you. Just stay here, okay?"

Scott bobbed his head with as much strength as he had, not like his frail body could actually carry him out of that dark room. Robin rushed out with Scott's note, "Thomas! Wait!"

Danielle and Carrie trudged their way to the basement door. It was practically falling off its hinges.

"Has anyone been down here since the place closed?" Danielle questioned. She and Carrie just stared at each other for a moment. "Are we really going to go down there by ourselves?"

"Do we have a choice?" Carrie asked. "I mean we have to finish this thing, and this is the best way to do it, so I mean, screw it." She reached for the doorknob and yanked it. It didn't budge. "Okay, maybe we won't be."

Danielle gave it a shot, "Help me, maybe we can do it together." Both women pulled hard on the door. It still refused to open.

"Um, what's that?" Carrie pointed to a deadbolt on the door.

"Shit, it's locked," Danielle shouted.

Carrie grabbed the flashlight from Danielle, "How about this?" She smashed the glass out of the fire extinguisher case. Carrie grabbed the extinguisher, "Here take this," she handed her the flashlight. Carrie raised the fire extinguisher above her head then smashed the deadbolt. "There," she held her hand out, "after you."

Danielle hesitantly opened the door, "I do not have a good feeling about this." She stepped down into the darkness.

The two women made their way down the rickety, old steps. "Are there no lights down here?" Carrie asked.

"Doesn't look like it," Danielle looked back up toward Carrie. "Here, hold on, I think I have another flashlight." She grabbed her backpack and reached in, "It should be in here…" she took another step down but tripped over the last step, Danielle fell hard on the concrete floor and Carrie slammed down right on top of her.

"What the hell was that?" Carrie screeched as she looked up from the dust covered floor.

"Oh shit, look at that," Danielle motioned back to the stairwell. A single strand of fishing string ran from one side of the stairs to the other.

"What the fuck?" Carrie yelled, "Who would do…" She trailed off as she glanced toward the boilers. "Oh shit!"

Danielle made her way to her feet. "Aaron?" She ran over to him. Aaron was pinned against the wall. Barbed wire wrapped around his arms, chest, and neck, each one cut into his flesh, blood seeped through each spot the rusted metal pressed against his body. Blood began to build up in a puddle around his feet and poured from his mouth. Behind him sat a blast furnace, the large door hung wide open.

"That thing couldn't have been used since this place closed but listen…" Carrie noticed the loud humming noise reverberating from that very furnace.

"The doctor is back, he did this!" Aaron shouted; blood squirted from his mouth.

"What?" Danielle pulled on the wire.

He writhed in agony, "No, don't pull it." More blood shot out of his mouth as he screamed. "I think they used tripwire to turn on the furnace or some shit."

"That doesn't even make sense; ghosts using tripwire?" Carrie bellowed. "Wait you said they? So, there was more than one?"

"The doctor and a…skull." More blood spewed from his mouth, "Take the phone and get out, it's too late for me. Just get out of here."

Danielle shook her head, "I won't leave you," she bent over to kiss him.

Carrie grabbed the phone out of his pocket and then grabbed Danielle, "Come on!" The furnace screeched louder and louder. "We got to go!"

Danielle fought against her, "No, I have to —" Flames spout out of the furnace, they enveloped Aaron. His clothing burnt and melted to his skin, his skin seemed to melt off with the extreme heat from the furnace. "Nooo!" Danielle screamed and fell backward.

Carrie picked her up, "Come on, we have to go!"

"Aaron! Please, no!" Danielle fought her way from Carrie's grasp. She ran over to Aaron. The fire had only shot out momentarily but had been enough to char his body and melt half of his skin completely off. "Aaron! I lo —"

He groaned, barely able to move his lips. His muscles and tendons showed through his charred flesh, and blood now seeped from every crevice of his tormented body. The now burning hot barbed wire had melted into his body as well, it dug deeper and deeper. "Leave," he muttered. The furnace hummed again, "I lo –" the flames poured out and once again engulfed him, this time it basically incinerated what was left of his body.

"Nooo!" Danielle was in tears.

"Let's go! Now!" Carrie once again grabbed Danielle and pulled her back. Danielle's screams echoed throughout the building, louder than Aaron's final painful, tortured screams.

Max ran down the basement stairs; nearly fell over the trip wire as he noticed at the last second. "What the hell happened?" he saw Carrie and Danielle huddled together at the bottom of the stairs.

After neither woman answered, he finally glanced toward the blast furnace and perceived what was left of Aaron's burnt, lifeless carcass.

Thomas followed directly behind Max. The color in his face drained as it turned pale just as Max's did. "What the hell?" He bent down, let out a few groans, and finally vomited upon the disgusting sight.

Without a word, Carrie and Danielle headed back up the stairs. After he composed himself, Thomas followed in their footsteps.

"Where are Robin and Scott?" Carrie glanced down to Max, then over to Thomas.

Thomas held his stomach, "Robin's watching over Scott. He had uh…uh an accident."

"What kind of accident?" Carrie seemed to panic.

"He had his tongue ripped out," Max declared quite blatantly.

Both women were held speechless.

"He's going to be fine though," Thomas assured them. "We just need to get him to a hospital."

"Did you get the phone off him?" Max asked the women.

Danielle nodded, "Yeah, we did."

"Is that all you care about?" Carrie demanded. "Getting out of here and making your damn money, right?"

Thomas continued up the stairs, "Come on guys, we need the phone to get Scott to a safer location."

The group maintained their hike up the unstable, shaky stairs.

"What the hell is that?" Thomas observed a strange, red light that flashes rapidly behind the basement door.

"Oh God," Danielle murmured.

"What is it?" Max insisted.

Thomas scowled, "Jesus…the building is in lockdown." He shoved open the basement door, only to disorienting spinning red lights which lined the ceiling of seemingly every room in the asylum. "Come on, we need to get to our wing."

"Good idea, the red lights probably weren't reconstructed in there," Carrie agreed.

"Hurry," Danielle whispered, "I think I'm going to be sick."

Derrick Smith

Chapter 10

YOU CAME?

"Come on Alex pick up," Thomas pleaded.

"Talk to me," Alex's voice boomed over the phone.

"Thank God. Alex, we need help. Scott's in trouble and now these damned red lights are spinning all around us, I think something triggered them."

A long pause ensued, "Okay, first off, what kind of trouble is he in?"

Thomas took a deep breath, "His tongue, it was…removed."

"Dear God…I…I"

"Just send help for him and he'll be okay," Thomas promised Alex. "We'll even finish the movie, just get him to safety."

Another pause, "I wish I could, but –"

"But what?" Thomas cut him off.

"Those red lights; they signify a full system lockdown. No one gets in…or out. All entrances are locked until the key switch is activated."

Thomas sighed and regained his composure, "Is there anything you can do?"

"I will personally visit the caretaker of this place, maybe he'll be able to give us a key or some shit."

"Thank you, Alex, I appreciate it. But please be as quick as possible, we don't have much time."

"Hopefully the weather holds up, it's really coming down. Half of the city's power is out. But as soon as I get an answer I will send medics and we'll take him to the TJU Hospital, about twenty minutes or so away."

"I'll try to comfort him until then; I just can't guarantee how long we'll have a full and willing crew after this though."

"Try to keep them in this, Tom. You really know how much we all need this."

Another sigh escaped Thomas, "Yeah, I really do. I'll keep everyone calm; I'll hopefully see you and some doctors soon."

"Be safe and keep rolling with the movie, I want this finished ASAP."

"You got it, just hurry."

After he took a brief moment to collect himself, Thomas turned back to the corridor which led to the rest of the crew.

"You two need to go to the church, and Carrie and I will search the violent hallway and all of those rooms," Max commanded.

The rest of the group did not seem too thrilled about his plan, but after all, he was brought in to help finish the movie and get them all out safely.

"What about Scott?" Carrie questioned. "He should be a priority shouldn't he?"

Danielle didn't make a sound; she curled in the fetal position on one of the mattresses. She could be heard muttering something under her breath repeatedly, "It's my fault…My fault…Oh God, Aaron."

"We need her," Max whispered to Carrie. "See if you can calm her the fuck down."

Carrie nodded, "But really, what about Scott? Shouldn't we get him out?"

"Well, Tommy boy should be taking care of that right…" he turned back to the door only to notice Thomas's silhouette outlined in the gloomy, red illumination just beyond it, "Now."

Carrie swung around, "Tom! Any word on getting Scott out of here?"

A grim look cultivated on Thomas's face, "Not exactly."

"What the hell does that mean?" Carrie demanded.

"Well, those red lights? They mean that we're in a full lockdown. All exits and entrances are sealed until the owner unlocks the door."

Max smirked, "Oh and let me guess…" he scoffed, "Alex is going to come through for us?" He laughed mercilessly.

"That's the plan, according to him," Thomas reassured them all.

The smile still pursed on Max's face, "Right, well it looks like it's up to us to find a way out; Alex never keeps his word."

"Great, that's just great news," Carrie mocked.

"Where's Robin?" Danielle suddenly spoke.

"Shit, I left her with Scott. She probably freaked out by now," Thomas jumped and turned back to the door. "I'll go get them both and bring them back here."

Danielle lifted herself to her feet, "I'm coming with you."

Thomas turned back, "No, I think we should all stay together actually."

"Um, I don't think so," Max argued. "I'm going to find a way out of here, and then maybe, just maybe we can get some help for the mute and little miss pretend."

Thomas grabbed his collar, "What the hell is your problem? Ever since you got here you've done nothing but break this group apart! Maybe it's you that did that to Scott! You never liked him; you never liked any of us. So how do we know that you're not going to try to knock off every one of us?"

"Fuck you! It wasn't my idea to come here! Alex wrote me a check for a half a million dollars to get you all out of here alive," Max shoved Thomas hard. He faltered backward. "And by God, that's exactly what I'm going to do!"

Thomas backed up and felt around for the door, he motioned for Danielle and Carrie, "Let's go get Scott and Robin."

Carrie shook her head, "No, I'm going with Max. He knows what he's doing."

Thomas seemed taken back, "We really all should stick together, Carrie."

Danielle nodded her head, "He's right, everyone that disappeared was left alone; you can't -"

"I think she can make up her own mind," Max elucidated. "Let's go find a way out of here."

Thomas and Danielle trudged down the red illuminated hallways, back towards the makeshift darkroom to where Thomas had left Robin and Scott.

"As soon as we get them back to the safe area," Thomas reached into his coat pocket for the emergency phone, "we'll call…"

"What is it?" Danielle murmured.

"I don't know where…"

"Max…that bastard!" Danielle shouted.

Thomas shook his head, "Son of a bitch, he stole the phone."

"Shit. What do we do now?"

"I don't know, I don't know, I don't know…" Thomas panicked.

Danielle stepped back, "Let's get Scott and Robin first, and then we can worry about finding Max and the phone. Okay?"

Thomas nodded, "Okay, let's hurry; we won't be able to find Max after a while."

The two continued to the dark room, almost in a slow jog.

Danielle paused, "Wait a sec. Why won't we be able to find him?"

"He used to have a tendency to…make an early exit without telling any of us. It was before you were with us," Thomas explained. "We just have to hurry and hope that Alex does come through."

"Come on, it's right there, one thing at a time," she inched the door open.

"Oh…my…" Thomas was dumbfounded. Blood was splattered on the floor, the walls, the ceiling. Scott lay on the ground, curled up in a ball. Dried blood perched on his lips, once again reminding everyone of his lack of tongue. Two ice pick- type utensils sat on the metal tray directly beside him.

"What the hell?" Carrie rotated to face the wall. The word 'Finish' was written completely in blood. "Jesus, whose blood is that?"

Thomas stepped back and grabbed Scott, "Come on, lets…" Scott's eyes were rolled in the back of his head, his eye sockets bruised with an almost fully black color; his arms had been wrapped behind him with a large white jacket. "A lobotomy…"

"What?" Danielle shrieked.

"Someone treated him as a crazy patient that needed surgery," Thomas pointed to the ice picks. "Those were used for frontal lobotomies."

Danielle was in shock, "So he's…he's…"

"Brain-dead," Thomas pulled Scott off the ground, "Let's get out of here."

"Where's Robin?"

"Son of a bitch!"

The laboratory door swung open, "Come on," Max shouted. He yanked Carrie inside.

"I thought we were trying to get out, not deeper into this place."

"I studied the most recent map on the way here with Alex. I think there's some sort of secret exit in here," Max circled the laboratory.

"Thank God, no red lights," Carrie shrugged. "I don't like this place; this is where Danielle was attacked." She gazed over to the center of the room where Danielle was seated, a large metal table, now coated with flasks and syringes. "That wasn't here before, what's going on?"

Max grabbed Carrie's arm and pulled her aggressively, "Come on, don't pay attention to little things like that. I'm sure Alex paid Robin extra to sneak away and scare the living piss out of us."

"But I just, I don't know if I can take much more of this."

"Relax, we'll find the trap door, and –" a loud thud echoed throughout the lab, "I think I found it." Max smiled and bent down. He shoveled off the dust and dirt that covered the hidden, metal door. "See; told you." He grabbed the handle and heaved. It wouldn't give.

"Here, let me help." She stepped over to him and clutched the groove in the floor and pulled it hard with Max.

The door finally gave way to sheer, seemingly never ending, darkness. "Follow close behind and keep low." They crawled into the darkness, and shuffled through as quickly as possible.

Scott rested at the entrance hall of the asylum while Thomas and Danielle tried the entrance. No such luck, it wouldn't budge.

"Let's try the glass over here," Thomas explained to Danielle.

They pounded on the reinforced glass repeatedly. Thomas pulled up a stray chair and tossed it against the large window. The chair smashed in about six pieces; the window was still intact.

"What the hell," Danielle groaned, "this is useless."

Thomas turned back to the window, "There's got to be a way to –" a shrewd strike against the glass startled both crew members. "What the _"

"Tom, I've been calling you!" the voice shouted but was barely heard through the reinforced glass and locked up metal door. "I couldn't get through! The owner is out of town and his phone is off!"

"Alex?" *You actually came?*, he thought. "How the hell do we get out of here? Scott's getting worse!"

"Can you break the glass?"

"Tried it," grumbled Danielle.

Thomas sighed and rolled his shoulders, "Any ideas? Max took Carrie and they're searching for ways out."

"According to the plans there are two…two…two…" Alex seemed to freeze.

"Two what? Two what?" Danielle screamed, nearly in tears, "Please, two what?"

"Alex! Alex! Are you alright?" Thomas hollered through the glass.

Alex took a step back, "Two…" He spun and dropped to his knees, a large, rusted knife was jammed into his spinal column, he coughed up a mouth full of blood, "Two…"

"Alex, no!" tears built up in Danielle's eyes, "No!"

"Shit, Alex!" Thomas glanced back at Danielle, now crouched down beside Scott. "Pick him up! We need to find a way to get out there!" He turned back to the window, "Alex, hold on!"

A tall figure stepped out of the darkness; it was cloaked in black except for the face. A grim, off-white skull seemed to grin at Thomas. It gazed down at Alex, he began to twitch and spat more blood. He held up his hand and lifted two fingers, "Two…" he groaned. "Ex –" A piercing screech shot through the reinforced window and door as the figure hauled Alex by his foot into the shadows. Thomas looked on in horror, not a clue what to do.

"Come on Danny!" Thomas ran over to her and Scott. He lifted her up, "Grab Scott, we need to get to that map and the phone!"

It seemed like an eternity, only twenty minutes, which Max and Carrie crawled in the obscure shadows. Finally, Max reached out and thrust open a round, rusted gate. At last, they were free.

"Come on Carrie!" Max turned back to pull her out of the tunnel, and shouted, "Carrie?" She had disappeared. He bowed down into the passageway, "Carrie!" He began to crawl back in, "Carrie!" He felt a tug at his shirt, "Carrie?" He was dragged violently back into the gloomy tunnel. His head slammed off some sort of object on the top of the passage. He lay on his back momentarily, "What the?" The object looked like a camera; Alex turned his head slightly. He perceived a dim lit skull-looking phantom. "Who —" he was dealt a swift blow to the head. He struggled temporarily until another strike to his head sent him into complete blackness.

Scott was seated on a rickety stool in the kitchen, Danielle and Thomas sat under the bright light over the kitchen table. Thomas pulled out the plans to the building and began to examine them.

"Look at this," he muttered. There seemed to be two unblocked exits: one through the chapel, the other an old mine shaft in the basement.

"That must be what Alex meant by two. Two exits."

"Which should we aim for?" Thomas asked Danielle.

Danielle thought for a moment, glanced back at Scott, "With Scott, I think it'd be easier to get through the chapel instead of hauling him downstairs."

"Good call; let's pack up everything we have in here that can help us."

Danielle grabbed the three stray flashlights, and a pack of batteries stashed in the cabinet. Thomas collected the two cameras left over from Scott and Aaron's dark room and the maps they had pulled out.

"Ready?" Thomas inquired.

"Let's get to the chapel," Danielle declared as she reached down to grab Scott. "Gimme a hand and we can get going."

"Lead the way!" Thomas proclaimed.

As Max awoke, he noticed Carrie strapped to a chair. It didn't appear to be any ordinary chair – no, it was an old-fashioned electric chair. Her arms and legs were strapped to the wooden legs of the torture device. "Carrie," he whispered, "Carrie, wake up."

She shook her head and slowly awoke. Carrie began to panic, "What...where are we?" She shook viciously and tried to free herself, "God, please, I don't want to die!"

Max's eyes opened extensively, "Wha..."

"What are you doing here?" a voice rumbled from behind Carrie.

Max stuttered, "We're...we're..."

"Filming a movie," Carrie stammered.

He shot her a wicked look, "We're investigating this building for paranormal activity."

"You disturbed the home of the innocent souls left behind," the voice roared. The figure swung around from behind Carrie to stare her directly in her eyes. The skull face of the figure seemed to outweigh the ringing of the voice in their ears.

Carrie's vision blurred, the skull seemed to pierce deep into her soul, "Sk…sk…skull."

"What do you want from us?" Max demanded; he showed no fear.

The seemingly undead beast revolved instantly for eye contact with Max, "Out. The only way to get out," it grabbed Max's jaw, "is for you to finish."

"What does that even mean?" Max asked as his eyes went blurry as well.

The skull figure did not reply, "Finish the job!" The black cloaked figure sauntered back behind Carrie, "I warn you all, only one may leave alive!"

"Why? I thought if we finished that we could leave?" Max bellowed.

"The only way out for you is to pull the lever," the voice boomed. It pointed to the charred handle about a foot away from Max's chair. The figure unlocked Max's left arm, "The quicker the better."

"No, no, I won't. I can't!" Max argued. He shook his head and reached over with his free arm; he pulled at his restraints.

"Don't!" The figure grasped Max's arm and slammed it back down and re-strapped the clamp on his wrist. It grabbed a large, shiny, surgery knife off an old, rusted laboratory table. "Maybe this will sway your decision." The figure bent down behind Max, "Shall I slice your ankles so you can no longer walk?"

Max squirmed in his restraints as the figure knelt down behind him. "Please! No!"

"No?" The figure stood. "Okay. I have a better idea anyway." It circled around Max held captive in his chair.

"What are you doing?" as tears nearly swelled up in his eyes.

The figure reappeared from behind Max's chair. A long, slender sledgehammer was clutched in his hand. "In that case, you will not walk out of here!" It pulled the rusted and splintered sledge back, over his head. The hammer slammed down on his left knee. Blood sprayed from his flesh as his kneecap crushed under the immense pressure of the weapon.

Max's screams echoed throughout the halls of the asylum.

"Change your mind yet?" It pulled the sledgehammer back over its shoulder.

"Fuck you!"

The sledgehammer crashed down on his right knee. "Fuck me? Oh no!" Its laughter boomed throughout the room. "Fuck you!" More laughter resonated from the figure as it stepped back.

Max writhed in pain but continued to shake his head, "You bastard!"

"It really does *not* need to be this difficult!"

Max's face puckered and twisted in sheer agony, "No, I won't!"

"She will die either way, by my hand or yours," the figure slammed the butt end of the knife into Max's temple. "You can join her, if you like," the knife slashed up and down Carrie's arms multiple times.

Max thrashed about in misery, "Noo! Please!"

"Put her out of her pain," the figure took the sharp blade to Carrie and began to hack away at her chest, arms, and face. It threw one blow after another, blood spout through each injury as she yelled louder at every slash.

"Please! No! No!" Carrie pleaded, "Please...please...please."

The figure once again released Max's arm. He reached over to the lever, "I'm sorry," he murmured, tears rolled down his cheeks. His hand shook juristically, "I can't. I just can't."

The being threw the switch suddenly and strode slowly into the darkness. Carrie's body thrashed and twitched back and forth drastically. Her skin began to blacken, and her eyes bulged from her head, smoke rose from her smoldered body. She continued to scream until finally, her body stopped; Carrie's skin was charred and nearly fell from her muscle, hair a crisp black color, and eyes nearly plunged out of her sockets.

"Help!" Max shouted for help from someone, anyone. "Please! Help!"

The figure appeared behind Max and lifted the knife above his shoulder. It brought in down and pierced Max's shoulder, then the other. The figure beat Max with the butt end of the knife until dark, black bruises covered his body, "Plea...sto...I cat..." His jaw was broken in multiple places, teeth were knocked out, and his arms were covered in warm, seeping blood from the wounds on his shoulders. It pained him to even move, his knees were weak from the blood loss and the excessive bruises down each leg. "Fu...yu," Max's arms fell limp to his side and his head fell cocked awkwardly. He could no longer feel his feet; there was too much pain to endure any longer. He needed rest if he were to escape the clutches of the evil that had murdered each investigator one by one.

The figure released Max's restraints. It then exited without another word, silently, and quickly. It had left Max for dead.

The chapel was in sight; Scott dragged along between Thomas and Danielle for the trek. He grew heavier with each step.

"Tom, I think he's —"

"Shit!"

Scott plunged to the concrete hallway floor; his body seemed stiff and rigid. His white jacket, now unstrapped from behind his back, spilled what was situated within – video tapes.

"Scott, you'll be okay," Danielle commented, not expecting a response.

Thomas bent down and grabbed Scott's shoulders, "Come on buddy. Let's get you back up." He sat Scott up against the brick wall which surrounded the chapel.

"What the hell?" Danielle snatched up the tapes that dropped out of Scott's jacket. "These are video tapes from Scott's camera. Why…how would he put them in here?"

"We'll watch them later; we need to find that exit in the church."

She stood with a tight grip on the tapes, "No, I really think we should watch them now."

After a moment, Thomas was reluctant to agree, "Yeah, you might be right. Maybe they can help us understand what's going on." He reached into his sack. Thomas drew out one of the small, handheld cameras they brought. "Here," he handed it to her, "we'll check it out when we get into the sanctuary of the chapel."

"Okay, works for me," Danielle nodded.

Thomas yanked Scott up off the wall, "You're okay; nice and slow now."

"Come on, come on, come on," Danielle grew impatient. She reached down and helped pull Scott up.

Thomas moved forward with Scott, one step at a time, "Okay, slowly." He budged open the door.

"Oh, what's that smell?" Danielle held her nose.

Thomas simply shook his head, "Not a clue." He looked around, "Come on, let's get to the front."

The trio slowly worked their way through the rotted, old pews and took a seat in the front row. "Okay, get out the tapes."

Danielle rustled through the backpack, finally drug out the tapes and handheld camera. "Here," she handed it over.

Thomas held it close, "Are we sure we want to see this?"

Danielle sat quietly and grabbed Scott's hand, "We've come this far," she sighed, "We can at least find out what all this is about."

Apparently Thomas agreed and tossed the video tapes into the camera and clicked the play button, "Well, here we go."

On his forearms, Max inched his way down the hall, back towards the chapel. "Help!" his voice was raspy and did not echo as he hoped it would. A long trail of blood led from the sanctuary room where he and Carrie were trapped. Both of Max's knees bled profusely and were stretched and contorted so juristically that he couldn't move them. Cuts spewed blood from his shoulders which had been torn open. Blood trickled down the corners of his lips from the beating he took from the butt end of the skull knife.

Beaten and battered from the knife wounds left by the skull encrusted, tattered cloak draped figure, which tortured and murdered Carrie right in front of his eyes, Max grew dizzy from the excessive blood loss. "Please!" He spat a mouth full of blood onto the floor, tears welled up in his eyes, "I don't want to die," he muttered.

A light gleamed in the distance, passed the red lights, toward the entrance of the moss-covered halls, a vivid beam shone through a doorway – it was the chapel! Cold overtook his entire body, "Hello…" his voice trailed off, unable to shout any longer. Max nearly gave up, flailed his head side to side in absolute pain. With one moment of heroism, Max breathed deep, dug into the floor with his fingernails, and dragged himself toward the chapel; a long, thick trail of warm, fresh blood was left behind him.

"I don't really think this hell hole is haunted, it's just in peoples' heads. The eerie sounds, just figments of imagination," Aaron proclaimed with strict confidence. He shook his head, "I just have a hard time believing some of the stories, you know?"

The picture cut out on the handheld camera; tears dripped from Danielle's eyes as she rubbed them away quickly. "Is that it?"

"It doesn't seem –" Thomas paused and stared blankly at the picture, "Wait!" He motioned back to the screen, "What the…"

A black figure turned away from the camera, Michael's tall, slender body lay, strapped down to the metal table. He fought against the straps and the figure. Michael squirmed and tried to scream but his mouth was gagged with a bloody cloth. The morgue table shook viciously, suddenly, the camera moved.

Danielle glanced toward Thomas, "Oh God."

The black figure held a knife, encrusted in skulls. It reached back and dealt multiple blows to Michael's midsection, then to his head. It left a bloody mess on the table, screams ricocheted about the morgue.

A muffled voice could be heard commanding the cloak wrapped figure from behind the camera. It looked directly into the camera, the blank, lifeless skull nodded, then pointed its knife toward the camera, then back across its neck, mimicking a slit throat. Then it lifted the sharp blade and swiftly plunged it into Michael's bowels. Slowly, it drove the knife deeper and deeper into his gut. The knife cut upward and formed a triangle in Michael's stomach to his rib cage. Michael writhed in pain and shrieked louder, louder, until he finally fell silent.

"He was alive while he slaughtered him…" Danielle trailed off in disbelief.

"They," Thomas calmly stated, "Someone picked up the camera too."

The picture drew close on Michael's carcass. The dark figure pulled out a gruesome needle, some old thread, and began to sew up the incisions. The camera grew closer to watch the horrific scene of inhumanity.

"I can't watch this," Danielle turned away from the picture.

"Mikey!" a voice shouted from behind them.

The camera man turned toward the door, and then back to the grisly torture scene, "Let's go!" the cameraman shrilly commanded.

The skull clad figure nodded, grabbed the knife and needle, and followed the cameraman out the other door. The camera's screen turned static and then went completely black.

"How could anyone do this?" Danielle questioned, as she held her stomach.

Thomas just shook his head, "I have no idea." He reached for another tape.

"What are you doing?"

"We need to keep searching for something that can lead us to who did this," Thomas demanded. He tossed another tape in the camera and then slammed the camera door. "You don't have to watch, you know."

Danielle shrugged, "I don't know how much more I can take, especially when it comes to -" she noticed Aaron on the floor of the basement lit up on the camera.

Aaron lay on the floor, shirt torn off. Scratches, cuts, and burns enveloped his body. His face was bruised and slightly cut, as though he were beaten with a blunt object. His eyebrows black and blue sliced just above the eyelid. His lips and cheeks blown up with bruises, carved up in crisscrosses. He groaned motionlessly as the camera drew closer and closer to the beaten victim.

The dark cloaked figure once again appeared on the screen, this time with an arm full of rusty barbed wire. It bent down and began to wrap Aaron's arms in the wire, he shrieked repeatedly.

"Pl…pl…please," he begged.

The cameraman once again closed in on the victim. "Stand him up," the voice commanded. The camera glanced over to the wall. A green clothed arm outstretched from behind the camera and pointed to a spot which sat directly in front of the furnace. "There!"

The skull-faced figure grabbed Aaron. It dragged the barbed wire wrapped around him and pulled him to the area in front of the furnace.

Danielle glanced quickly at the picture on the camera, "Oh Jesus, that's where we found him!" She shook her hand and grabbed her stomach, "I can't…I just," she bent over and let out a loud heave.

The figure pulled the wire tighter around Aaron's arms, legs, and neck. It began to cut deeper, deeper…the picture adjusted to static once again.

"Damn," Thomas muttered. "I thought…wait," he looked back down at the screen.

It cut back in, this time it was shot from behind Danielle and Carrie. It zoomed close into Aaron wrapped in barbed wire and just glared on as he thrashed about in pain. The fire could be heard building up in the background, then suddenly poured out from behind Aaron, once again charring his body.

"Shut it off!" Danielle yanked the camera away from Thomas. "I just can't watch that again!"

Thomas glanced down then took hold of her hand, "I understand. Can you take the tape out? I'm going to save all these; I think they could be used as evidence."

Danielle just nodded and handed the tape over, "I can't watch anymore now, please."

"That's fine," Thomas stuffed the tapes into his bag. "Let's try to find this hidden exit." He stood from the pew and strolled up to the altar and made his way behind the fallen podium. The fake body still lay under it, the blood, cornstarch and food coloring, still resting in a slight puddle around the podium. It did fall down some cracks in the floor, thus giving a vivid outline of a square.

"Come look at this, Danny," Thomas bent down and outlined the shape with his fingers.

She stopped about a foot away from the puddle of fake blood, "Is that it?"
"I'm guessing," he shrugged his shoulders, "Do you see a handle?"

"Um, is that it?" Danielle pointed to a small indent in the wood, just large enough for a hand to fit under.

A smile grew on his face, "Thank God!" He managed to work it up, the blood drained off and the dust seemed to just disintegrate into the thick air. "What was that?" He looked back to the entrance of the chapel, Thomas pointed back to the door. "Did you hear that?"

Danielle shook her head quickly, "No, we don't have time. Let's just get the hell out of here."

Thomas jumped down off the altar. He walked past the pews and Scott who sat in complete silence and a little drool falling down his mouth. Thomas rushed to the door and then paused. He glanced back toward Danielle who struggled to pull Scott up off the pew but was unable to lift him. He took a deep breath, clutched the handle, and pulled with all his might.

Max finally arrived at the door of the chapel; the light shone through the cracks. *Thank God,* he thought, *finally a safe haven.* He managed to crawl his way up to the long, high door handle with his arms alone. Max lost his grip and fell back to the concrete. He looked up from his place on the floor, Max noticed that he managed to crack the door open. He worked his way up to the wall and sat for a moment to gain his strength. "Finally," he muttered.

He rolled over on his stomach and crawled through the doorway, it looked a lot larger than last time. Max looked down the aisle, someone was storming toward him. "No! Not again, ple –" he was cut off instantly, darkness enveloped him. Cold was the last sensation Max felt.

"What the hell?" Thomas jumped back. He thought he had beaten the hell out of the *killer.* "Oh God, Max?"

Max had shards of the plastic camera stuck in the side of his head. On top of that, both of his knees were bleeding profusely; his head had been beaten in, it was battered, bruised, and bloody.

"What happened?" Danielle shouted from the front of the church.

No answer, Thomas just stood and stared at the lifeless body. Danielle placed a hand on Scott's back while he sat in the pew. "Stay here," she whispered. She rushed over to Thomas, tears dripped down her cheeks, "What happened?"

Thomas stammered nervously, "He asked for mercy. The killer didn't give any of us mercy, why should I give him any?"

"But it's Max! How could you?"

Thomas turned back to the door and slammed it shut, "I was trying to protect us! I didn't know it was Max! How could I? It's dark, I was scared. I just want to leave."

Danielle bent down to Max, "No pulse."

"What's that?" Thomas grabbed Max's arm. There was a word carved into it, blood spilled from every wound. "Cellar?"

Danielle pursed her lips, "What the hell?"

"I think…" he trailed off. Thomas twisted his other arm, "Wait, look…"

Another word pierced his arm; 'Finish' was spelled out and bled just as severely.

"Oh shit!" Danielle jumped back. "What the hell does that mean?"

"I think…I think they want us to finish whatever *it* is in the cellar."
Thomas stood and walked over to Scott and grabbed his arm, "Come
on buddy, we got to head to the basement."

"What?" Danielle demanded. "No, absolutely not."

Thomas continued to the door, "We have to face this. They won't let
us out until we do what they command."

She wiped the tears away from her eyes, "So what? Kill them?"

"No, we'll talk. We'll make a deal. Something, I don't know yet,"
Thomas pushed Scott against the wall. "Get the phone," he
commanded.

"From him?" she pointed toward Max. The tears began to roll down
her cheeks.

Thomas bent down to Max, "Fine, I'll find it." He searched through
his pockets, no phone. He dragged out more tapes, from Max's pocket
this time, "My God, Danny…Everyone's dead."

Chapter 11

WHO...WHAT...HOW

The picture seemed different this time. The previous tapes seemed to be filmed in a controlled environment; this one tended to be rushed and was located outside of the asylum. The wind whistled through the leaves, screams from inside of the building could be heard on the screen.

"Oh God," Thomas bellowed. "It's Alex's tape."

Danielle's face contorted, "Wait, what?"

Thomas merely pointed back down to the camera's screen. The back of Alex came into sight, as well as the black figure. The camera moved close, directly behind the skull figure as it raised its arm high, a knife fixed in its right hand. The figure plunged the knife into Alex's unsuspecting back. He fell in a heap, but still tried to tell Thomas something, whose head could be seen through the window.

Thomas shook his head and stared at the screen in disbelief, "The killer was watching us the entire time."

Danielle's dark, black eyes were fixed to the horror on the tape, "Why did he tape it?"

"I don't know, but he just stood there and stared at us," Thomas whispered. "He was mocking us."

The figure continued to stare at the pair inside the asylum. Alex was abruptly pulled into the darkness, not by the figure like they originally thought, but by the cameraman.

"This is no ghost," Thomas assumed.

"No," Danielle disagreed. "No person could do such a thing. That is a monster!"

Thomas trembled, "Give me the next one."

"I can't take this shit, "Here." She handed him another tape from the stash pulled from Max's pocket.

The screen snapped to life with the push of a little red button. Darkness filled the screen; the four walls of a room could finally be made out, along with two separate chairs which faced one another. Each was occupied by a victim.

"It's Max!" Danielle proclaimed.

"Who's the other?" Thomas asked, as the face could not even be recognized.

The figure appeared behind the unrecognizable individual. Its voice cut through the air but could not be distinguished through the tape. The skull clad figure worked its way over to Max who was in much pain, writhing and squirming about. It bent low, released his right arm from the chair, and apparently whispered into his ear, for Max instantly shouted "No!" and twisted even more.

Danielle covered her mouth, "Shit."

The figure must not have taken kindly to his response; it shackled him back in and began to beat him profusely. Blood splattered all over; on the chairs, the walls, even the camera. Blood drops trickled down the camera, Thomas and Danielle winced at the sight. The cameraman quickly wiped away the streaks left of Max's blood.

"It's Carrie!" Thomas abruptly shouted, "Shit, that's Carrie."

Danielle panicked, "We got to get out of here. Please, can we go, please, please…?" She broke down in tears.

Thomas held her tight and comforted her, "It's okay, we'll go. We'll go." Once again, he fixed his eyes on the camera.

The figure strolled back behind Carrie, again barked out to Max. It raised its arm high, then released. The blade penetrated deep into Carrie's chest. It withdrew the knife and then pierced her once more. This time, it twisted the knife, she spat up a lung full of blood.

"Oh, dear lord…"Danielle muttered.

Once again, the figure strode to Max, loosened his left arm, and placed it on what looked like a lever.

Thomas shivered, "It wants him to pull the lever."

He refused repeatedly; the figure grew impatient. It bent low, grabbed out the blade, held it to Max's ankles, and then withdrew. It circled him and reached for something – a sledgehammer. It smashed both knees one after the other. Each time, blood shot out as Max screamed in pain. The figure grabbed hold of the rusted lever and slammed it down. Carrie's body twitched and shook viciously. Her body charred as Max was forced to watch. Everything went black.

Thomas clicked off the camera, "Okay, that's enough."

"I don't know how much more I can handle," Danielle clutched her stomach.

"Help me with Scott," Thomas had an arm around him.

The pair forced him up to his feet. They moved slowly to the chapel door, stepping over Max's cadaver. Thomas kicked the unhinged door open.

"Here, take the camera," Danielle handed it to Thomas.

He grabbed it and stuffed it in his backpack and pulled out the asylum floor plan. "Come on, the basement door is this way." Thomas packed the map away and grabbed a hold of Scott. He led the way with Danielle supporting him on the opposite side.

Scott once again was drugged between the two paranormal investigators. One of each of their arms around his back to support his weight, both of his legs scraped along the floor. After only five minutes of lugging Scott around the red silhouetted walls of the asylum, Danielle began to slip. She stopped and began to topple backward.

"Whoa," Thomas placed his hand on her back and heaved forward. "You okay?"

After she regained her composure she replaced her arm around Scott, "Yeah, yeah, I'm fine. I was just thinking though…"

"You shouldn't think too much about this shit right now," he assured her, "It's just too –"

She cut him off suddenly, "No, no, I mean about Robin. Where'd she disappear to?"

"I wish I knew," he concurred. "I haven't really even thought about her to tell you the truth, I guess I've been too worried about Scott and the phone and just getting the hell out of here."

Danielle snickered, "Yeah, you can't be blamed for that. I mean it's natural; what do they call it? Self-preservation, right?"

Thomas nodded, "Yeah, I think so. But do you think…eh, never mind."

"What?"

"Forget about it, really. It was nothing."

Danielle stopped and glanced over to him, "What? That it was Robin?"

"What? How could you…" he shot her a wicked look but then eased up. "Well, okay. I was actually beginning to think that, yeah." They stepped forward again; striding past the molded walls and boarded up windows.

"I don't know what to think though," Danielle thought out loud. "I mean, she's a special effects expert, not a murderer."

Thomas bobbed his head, "Think about that though. The effects all worked in favor of Ro – er uh, the killer. Every time something happened, the special effects had some part of it."

"Very true," Danielle agreed. "She did get this job because of her sick, twisted mind. I mean she really didn't care about the show at all, she just wanted the payday."

"Uh...yeah," Thomas answered uneasily. "She wasn't there for any of the murders was she? I mean, I still don't know though. This seems crazy, I mean, I almost married her."

"Wait, you almost what?"

Thomas shook his head, "Shit...well, we were engaged."

"Oh Jesus," Danielle stopped, "That's even more of a reason to get back at you."

"Well, it would be if I broke it off."

"Oh," she paused, then continued down the hall, "I'm sorry."

Thomas strolled alongside her and Scott, "Don't be." He shook his head, "It was for the best." Silence grew between the two, or well three of them. "Still, I don't know about the whole killing thing; I don't think she could hurt a fly, let alone another human being."

"Who then?" Danielle questioned. "We kind of need to figure everything out, or at least a way to combat her...him...them."

"You're right about that," they continued passing doors upon doors of empty, boarded up mental patients' rooms. "From the sounds of it, we're heading down to face the killer. So how do we get out of this?"

"Aren't there any other ways out? I mean, shouldn't this be the last resort?"

He seemed irritated, "Have you paid attention to any of this? Whoever is doing this knows their way around this place. They will find a way to kill us too." Thomas stopped yet again, "This way," the threesome turned the corner.

"So how do we beat them? Overpower them?"

"No, they obviously are strong. They have overpowered nearly every victim in one way or another," Thomas glanced over to Danielle. "Do we have any weapons?"

"Just what's lying around here, I guess. I don't know how much good that would do though if we can't out power them anyway. What's left? Outsmart them?"

Thomas fell silent momentarily, "I don't know, that might be tough too. They sort of outsmarted us the whole time, didn't they?"

"I guess so, knocking us off one by one, recording us incognito."

"So how do you outsmart a genius and execute a murderer?" Thomas riddled.

The group arrived at a large, wooden door. "I guess we're out of time," Danielle declared.

"No more time to think, "Thomas agreed, "Now it's time to act."

They descended the insecure stairwell slowly, cautiously. Danielle and Thomas both wrapped an outstretched arm around Scott. The very few lights in the basement began to flicker, faster now.

"It's probably from the storm Alex mentioned earlier," Thomas assumed.

Danielle seemed uneasy, "But we have a generator, I don't think the weather has anything to do with a generator, does it?"

They finally reached the base of the stairs. The boiler could be seen directly in front of where they stood. Aaron's charred and lifeless body was still strapped to the wall in rusted barbed wire in front of the oversized boiler.

"What's that?" Thomas squinted in the strobe lights. He pointed behind Aaron, an aged, corroded, metal stood propped open on its hinges.

Danielle seemed to perk up, "An exit?"

"Seems too simple, but it's worth a shot," Thomas held his head high.

They dragged Scott to the entryway of the recently uncovered door. Danielle and Thomas had a slight glimpse of survival.

"Can you hold him up for a sec?" Thomas asked.

Danielle sighed but reluctantly nodded her head.

He tried to nudge open the door. It seemed too heavy to open. "Damn! I can't get it."

Danielle set Scott down on the floor, "Um, here," she reached down to the ground. She handed him a large, sign post looking object. "Give that a shot."

Thomas wedged the post in between the massive door and the dusty, collapsing wall. He put all of his weight and energy into it. It shifted just enough, "There, I think we can get it." The room revealed nothing but shadows and darkness.

"Here," Danielle tossed Thomas a flashlight, "You might need this."

He flashed her a smirk, "Thanks." Thomas thrust his head through the slightly opened door. The room was pitch black, no flickering lights, no spinning red illuminants. A whimpering reverberated from inside the room; he was momentarily frozen in fear.

"Tom?" Danielle was worried, "Everything okay?"

He nodded, not realizing she could no longer see him. The glow from the flashlight burst into the room. A single chair was situated turned away from Thomas. Someone was strapped to it! *Oh no, not again*, he thought. He inched closer, one step at a time, "Robin?" he whispered.

The captive could only whimper continuously.

Thomas grew closer; he placed his hand on the back of the chair.

"Thomas!" Danielle now demanded, "Is everything okay?"

He jumped, very startled. "Danielle…" he swallowed hard, "there's someone in here."

"What?" she grabbed Scott and pulled him in behind her. "Is that -?"

"Alex's doctor…" Thomas shone the flashlight on the hostage.

Danielle rushed to him as swiftly as possible with Scott still at her side. "Wait, what?"

Thomas bent low, shined the light toward the doctor, "Are you –"

The doctor's eyes were rolled to the back of his head; blood seeped from his hairline.

"What is it, Tom?"

"His eyes...his head...I think he's..." Thomas stammered.

"He's what? What is it?" Danielle once more began to panic.

Thomas glanced over toward Danielle, not sure how to explain. He reached for the doctor's apparent head injury. "I think..." he grabbed hold of the doctor's hair.

"Wait, what are you doing?"

He yanked on the hair. It stuck momentarily, and then it abruptly gave way to reveal a fresh layer of membrane draped over the doctor's still functioning brain.

Both Thomas and Danielle jumped back in horror.

"Jesus!" Thomas was overwhelmed.

Danielle fell backward on top of Scott, "Holy shit...what the hell...who would?"

The lights suddenly flashed on and the door slammed shut simultaneously. Danielle and Thomas huddled low and covered their faces with their battered and bruised arms. Scott lay on the cold, hard ground still in a flabbergasted stupor.

"Are you guys alright?" Thomas found his footing after minutes of frustration. He stumbled to where they had fallen. "Danny?"

She was unconscious, her arms crisscrossed, legs tangled; blood dripped from a blotch on her neck.

"Son of a…" he circled around. He remembered the same injury on Michael's neck, and again the first time Danielle had been drugged. "Stay back! I know you're here!" Thomas began to grow lightheaded, his vision blurred. "I know…I know…" he reached up for his neck. His hand trembled as it, as well as his neck, grew bloody just as Danielle's had been. "No!" Thomas spun around and then fell to the ground in a heap. Everything was turning black; he managed to thrust himself on his back. The skull face lagged in his memory as he lost consciousness, slowly, slowly.

Thomas rolled over, his eyes a little heavy. He inched to the side of his bed and made his way to his feet. *What the hell? It was a dream?* He thought. Thomas reached for his neck, no blood. His arms were no longer bruised, "Son of a bitch." He chuckled and walked to his bedroom door.

He reached for the doorknob but could not grab it. It was right in front of him, only inches away. "What the hell?" He pounded on the door, "Let me out!"

Some sort of invisible wall blocked out any possibility of him reaching the doorknob. He began to panic, "No! Let me out!"

The walls suddenly closed in on him, all four sides slammed against his body. He was enclosed in a tight box and was laid on his back.

"What the fuck?" Thomas shouted. "Let me out! Please!" He slammed his fists against the tightly compacted wood. He squirmed anxiously; the box closed in tighter. Thomas continued to kick and punch until finally the box gave way.

He pulled himself up in hopes to jump out of the box. "What the hell is this?" as he stared ahead. Immense heat consumed him, Thomas finally detected where the high temperatures resonated from. The entire area around the box began to glow a soft orange. The area surrounding the box was a large crematory! Flames engulfed the box from all sides, Thomas's skin began to burn immensely, he felt his thick hair begin to smolder from the heat, and it felt as though it were going to melt right off his bones.

His screams barely abscond from his box. Thomas glanced down, his legs melted completely apart from his torso, the box had disappeared, there seemed to be no escape.

The flames faded away just as quickly as they materialized, he appeared to be hallucinating. His eyes again bolted open, Thomas in a stupor, "What...I..."

He plunged into a dark, watery pit. Thomas could not breathe; he was submerged deep into the fluid. His lungs filled up the dark water. After nearly five full minutes of being immersed, he was released. Thomas grabbed for a ledge of the tub, he struggled for breath. He finally emerged from his watery grave. Once he sat on the ledge he gazed endlessly into the tub.

"No! No! No!" Thomas seemed alarmed as he saw the murky water had affixed to his skin. The fluid was grimy and sticky, "Blood, oh shit! It's blood!"

Thomas slipped off the ledge and fell back into the shadowy, bloody drum. He thrashed about until the blood filled his lungs. Darkness surrounded him as he plummeted into the shadows, with no end in sight.

He snapped awake. "A dream," he muttered. "It was just a dream…" Thomas trailed off then squirmed and twisted. Pain shot up his legs, down his arms, and pounded in his head. His eyesight a little fuzzy, Thomas tried to stand but his body refused to budge. His arms were pulled behind his back; a thick rope secured them in a tight knot. Thomas's feet were restrained to the legs of the chair he was secured against.

His attention quickly turned to a groaning noise originating from behind him. Thomas twisted slowly, "Hello?" His voice was somewhat scratchy.

Scott moaned while curled in the fetal position in the rear corner of the still tremendously bright room. His arms wrapped around his knees and twitched rigorously; blood droplets still managed to escape the corners of his mouth.

Thomas then turned his hazed vision directly in front of him, the doctor still fastened to his chair. The doctor's head rolled left, then right, then left once more. This process continued perpetually, blood trickled down from his severed scalp. A small, metal tray laid next to him, rusted, old instruments set on it.

"Danielle?" he bellowed, "Where are you?" Thomas squirmed yet again; his wrists grew red and bloody. He could not locate her; Thomas twisted his neck numerous times to try to find her.

Still, she was nowhere to be found.

The door slammed open abruptly. Outside the room, all lights seemed to be shut off. Darkness consumed all life outside of those walls. The large, cloaked, skull bearing figure soared into the room swiftly, contentedly.

Thomas was finally able to fully perceive the figure he had observed in the video tapes. A faded hood shrouded the figure's head, a half-skull mask which enveloped the top fraction of its face, and the bottom had been draped in a black cloth, almost like a bandana, with the nostrils and jaw of a skull painted upon the fabric. The figure's eyes, a dark gray color, pierced deep into his soul. Thomas was in awe as he was face to face with the murderer of his team.

Rage filled his thoughts, all of the murders that had taken place, all of the innocent lives stolen. Thomas struggled profusely; the arms of his chair began to collect tiny puddles of blood, originating from his now gushing wrists. "You bastard! Who the hell are you? Why the fuck are you –"

A tripod ripped across Thomas's face, tearing a gash into his cheek. Without a word, not even a sound, the figure propped the blood-spattered tripod up in the opposite corner of Scott. It stared directly at Thomas, the red light flashed on as the figure sauntered toward him.

Thomas licked his lip, where blood had seeped from the open cheek, "What are you doing?" he screeched. "What's going on?"

"Finish this!" the figure boomed. It strolled behind the doctor, placed a dirty hand on his head. It squeezed tight and grabbed a handful of hair.

"What does that mean?" Thomas demanded. "I don't know what you want!"

"Finish this!" The figure yanked hard on the doctor's scalp, the doctor's head fell to the side, blood trickled down the corner of his mouth, bloody mucus dripped from his unprotected brain.

"No! Leave him alone!" Thomas cried.

The scalp landed on his lap; blood seeped into his already dark jeans. The figure then clutched a rusted, sharp, scalpel from the metal tray beside the doctor.

"Fuck you!" Thomas screamed, "What do you want with us?"

It then seized a pair of scissors from that same table, moved the instruments up to the doctor's unprotected cranium.

Thomas squirmed much more, "No, you son of a bitch! Don't!"

"Finish it!" the figure agitatedly demanded once again. It took the scalpel into the doctor's brain, fished up a strand of brain tissue, and snipped it with the scissors. The doctor fidgeted only slightly, obviously unable to feel much at all, his face began to twist unnaturally; his body began to spasm viciously. "It's amazing how the human body works, isn't it?"

Silence.

"If you remove part of the brain, the rest can still survive."

"No...no...no...look at him. Oh Jesus...Oh God" Thomas bellowed; tears rolled down his cheeks.

"Just wait," the figure announced with great confidence. It sauntered behind Thomas with a small piece of the doctor's brain.

"What are you doing? What the fuck are you doing?" Thomas insisted. He coiled his head backward; the figure nonchalantly fed the chunk to Scott, who gorged it down without thinking twice.

The figure glared at Thomas, "See, Scott likes it." Its laughter filled the room.

Thomas's cheeks turned pale, "How could you..." he choked up a mouthful of vomit before he felt another pinch in his neck. His eyes grew blurry, his head dizzy as it collapsed to the side, and finally blacked out altogether.

As Thomas once again came to, he noticed the doctor hunched over in his chair, only partial brain matter had been left in his half vacant skull. Scott was on the floor gnawing on some of the remnants of the doctor's mind. The figure was no longer present in the intensely bright area where the three were trapped.

"Scott," Thomas whispered.

He managed to lift his head upward, directly to Thomas, but only to continue chomping on the doctor's brain substance. His mouth transformed into a dark red color from the top of the doctor's skull resting in it. The knife stuck in the metal tray; blood still trickled down the blade.

Thomas attempting to squirm out of his restraints slowly made his way through the rope. "Hello?" he announced, "Is anyone there?" *We're going to be stuck here for…for eternity*, he thought. Thomas continued to work his hands free, almost…

The door slammed open; a woman, covered in blood, head to toe, barged into the room.

"Robin?" Thomas's voice echoed throughout the room. "Robin, are you okay?" He struggled in his chair, nearly toppling it over.

Her shirt was covered in dark blood, dripped down to her soaked pants and shoes. She left a blood streak behind her with every step she took. Robin had a strong limp and dragged her left leg behind her right. "Braaaainnnss…" she uttered. Moans continued to escape her body, over and over.

"Robin! Thank God!"

She limped over to the doctor and bent down to him, her mouth agape, and ready to take a large chunk of his neck.

"What the hell?" Thomas shouted in pure confusion. "Robin! Stop!"

Robin instantly stood erect; she glazed directly into his eyes. Her head cocked to the side, "Finish it!"

Thomas's eyes opened wide, "What? What happened to you?"

She reached for the tray. Robin wrenched the skull encrusted knife out of the metal tray. "Finish it!"

"Finish what, finish what?" he raved.

Robin elevated the knife, and then suddenly, it crashed down into the doctor's chest.

"No! No! What are you doing?"

She entwined the knife in his chest; the doctor did nothing but mildly shudder as his body shut down once and for all. "I said finish it!" Robin turned her attention to Thomas. Blood squirted from the doctor's mouth, down his chest where the knife was still fused to his torso.

"Stop!" Thomas shrieked. "Why Robin? Why?"

Robin jerked the knife out of the doctor's chest, blood spewed from the open wound. She marched toward him, and bent low, "Take the knife," she whispered solemnly.

He shot a confused look. "Wait, wh —"

"He told me I could live if I did what he asked," Robin explained quietly. She placed the knife in his hand, still tied behind his back as she bent low and kissed his cheek discreetly.

"Who? Who is doing this?" his eyes grew wide as he gazed past Robin. "Shit, it's —"

Robin swung around; the figure stood gravely in the doorway. Not one word, his black eyes cut through the air.

Thomas frantically sawed through the rope behind his back.

The figure stepped forward, "Finish th –"

"Fuck you!" Robin shouted. "You finish this!"

The figure swiftly rushed Robin, who now stood defenseless. It reached for her throat with both hands and squeezed tight. She coughed up a stream of blood, she tried to scream but no words came out, just jumbled words. It had crushed her larynx!

"Shit," Thomas mumbled. "Shit, shit, shit," the ropes from behind him fell to the ground. He began to slice through the ropes which bound his leg.

Robin was thrown on top of the doctor, the figure pounced. It tore the doctor from the chair, trapping Robin underneath him. The figure grabbed the chair and smashed it against the wall. A splintered chair leg lay on the ground next to the skull bearing figure. It cocked its head to the side, grasped hold of the fragmented piece of lumber. The figure pulled Robin up with one sole hand by the hair. She flew up from under the doctor, her face filled with terror, eyes wide and dilated.

Thomas struggled with his leg restraints. The rope did not seem to give.

Without hesitation, the figure grabbed a handful of Robin's curly, dirty blonde hair, and pulled back brutally. She was completely helpless; the skull-clad figure grabbed Robin's jaw and pried her mouth open. It then turned the sharp, jagged edge toward her, "I gave you a deal and you didn't follow through. You won't ever be able to say another word!" It plunged the jagged wood into her mouth, blood spurting around the abrasion. The timber splintered the entire way down her throat. It applied more pressure; Robin gagged and coughed up more blood. Her eyes grew red, nostrils and mouth seeped blood. The wood finally broke through her neck, shot blood out all over the figure's cloak. Robin toppled to the floor without much more than a mumble and partial scream.

"Robin!" Thomas just broke free of his leg straps and jumped to his feet. "You son of a bitch! Why would you do this?"

The figure turned and gazed directly at him. It cracked its neck then its fingers, "You didn't finish it!"

Without another word, Thomas charged toward the masked figure. He tackled it into the tripod. Thomas shot back to his feet and clutched the collapsed tripod. "Here's your end, you mother fucker!" He raised it above his head, about to crash it down into the figure's gut.

The door ripped open and Danielle tore into the room. She pulled him out of the room, "Come on!" Scott had already been dragged out into the hall. "We need to get out of here! I found a way out!"

Chapter 12

AND THEN THERE WERE THREE

The threesome once more ventured down the convalescent hallways, again hoping to find an exit to their nightmarish exploration. Scott's feet dragged along the ground as the only surviving members of the paranormal investigation team pulled him along with them. All three battered and bruised from their supposed simple investigation that would one day make them rich and famous. Blood dripped from Thomas's wrists and ankles from the rope restraints which bound him to the horrible chair for the skull bearing figure's pleasure. His cheek gashed wide open by the tripod wielded by that figure. Scott, practically incapacitated by the apparent lobotomy performed on him. Blood still built up around his eyes and he was unable to prevent the drool from dripping down his mouth. Danielle had a slight limp to her walk but seemed to shrug it off as they all attempted to make their escape.

Thomas glanced over to Danielle, looking over Scott's limp body, "How did you get out of there?"

"I crawled out after you passed out from whatever shot he pricked you with," she shook her head as they picked up the pace. "I heard him and Robin discussing what they had planned for you; I tried to hurry as —"

"Wait, wait," Thomas stopped her. "This was planned? It sounded like Robin didn't have a choice. That she was just trying to make a deal to get her out of here in one piece."

Danielle quivered, "I think that was planned. They said something about deceiving you."

"But he killed her! He fucking killed her!"

"Maybe she had second thoughts. I don't know really, I just know that I heard them scheming," Danielle protested. "Don't feel bad for what happened; she was going to embalm you…alive."

Thomas's entire body shuddered at the sound of that torture, "I just think it's amazing how you got out of there without them knowing."

"I think they did, but they wanted you. They said something about…fini –"

"Finish it. Finish it, that's all I've been hearing. Finish what?"

Danielle stopped in her footsteps, "The movie. Finish what we came here to do."

"Why though? Could you tell who it was under that mask?"

"No, he…she…it had some sort of voice disguise. But as soon as I got out of that damned room, I stayed behind the door to listen to their plans," Danielle explained as they continued down the still flickering, half disintegrated corridor. "But as soon as I heard them talking about terrorizing you, I ran to find a way out."

"And?" Thomas retorted, "Did you?"

"I came back to get you, didn't I?"

"Not like I needed it," Thomas bickered. "I had that thing on its back, I could have killed it."

Danielle glanced down a side corridor, "That way." She led the group. "How do you know he didn't have you right where he wanted you?"

"I…I guess I don't."

"There," Danielle pointed to a bookshelf, half collapsed at the end of the hall.

Thomas rushed for it, "Wait, this?" He felt up the shelf, books practically crumbled to dust as he ran his fingers over them. "How –"

Danielle set Scott against an adjacent wall, "Yes, here." She grabbed a lever next to the bookshelf. Danielle yanked hard, the large, wooden piece of furniture slowly pushed outward, away from the wall. A rush of air shot out around the frame.

Thomas stood, mouth agape, not a clue what to think.

As Danielle pushed the bookshelf aside, a large, steel door appeared in its place. "I think it's an old fallout shelter built beneath the building right before it closed."

"You don't think it's another insane torture room?" Thomas questioned, a little hesitant.

Danielle shrugged her shoulders, "I doubt it. It seems too…new, unused, you know?"

"I suppose," Thomas grabbed Scott up from the floor. "We don't have too much of a choice, do we?" He stepped forward, "You're sure this leads outside?"

"Every shelter has multiple escape routes." She yanked on the lever, it was slightly rusted; much like the rest of the old building. "Shit, wait!"

"What? What is it?" Thomas dreaded that the figure followed them.

"Evidence," she uttered.

"Evidence for what?"

"Evidence so we don't get blamed for this massacre!"

Thomas looked down toward the dust covered concrete, "I...You know, you have a point. They could have been setting us up the whole damn time. How the hell can we get evidence though?"

"The cameras," Danielle outburst, "they show us all with the killer at one point or another. I'm sure that would be enough!"

Thomas sighed, "Son of a bitch! You're right, we need those tapes too."

"So what?" she asked, "We storm the castle? Run in and grab the tapes and run back out?"

"That'll be kind of hard with Scott attached to our side," Thomas declared. "Either way, I don't think that plan will work too well."

Danielle shot him a nasty look, "I was being facetious. But we can leave Scott here no matter what we do. You know he won't go anywhere. We can hide him in the vault."

"Okay, okay, so how do we get the cameras?" he questioned, still quite hesitant.

"Well, incognito I guess. We just will have to use the shadows and move quietly," she suggested.

Thomas finally nodded in acceptance, "Okay, let's get moving before it finds the tapes."

"You're right, let's get Scott in there," she pointed back to the cold, steel door. "Give me a hand would you?"

Thomas cautiously strolled back toward Scott, "Come on buddy, we're going to let you sit right here." He managed to raise Scott to his feet.

Danielle rushed over to the pair, "Here, let me help." She wrapped her arm around Scott's shoulders, her hand brushing against Thomas's, their eyes met for a split second. Hope suddenly filled both of their hearts.

"Let's do this," Thomas proclaimed as they both set Scott in the shelter. Together, they slammed the door, locking Scott in the unknown area indefinitely.

They retraced their footsteps back down the hallways where they had just escaped. The two slowly crept in the darkness, in search of their two handheld cameras and multiple tapes. They finally reached the secret room where the doctor and Robin had met their demise, as well as the last place either Thomas or Danielle remembered leaving the tapes.

"They should be here, right here!" Thomas whispered, nearly panicking. The tapes were missing, but the lifeless, bloody body of Alex's doctor was still laid by the chair. "Were they not here?"

"I…I think so," Danielle stammered.

Thomas reached down under the chair he was restrained in, "Nothing."

"Shit, wait…"

"Wait for what?" Thomas demanded. "We wait much longer, we aren't getting out of here."

Danielle scratched her head, "You know," she paused.

"What, what, spit it out?" Thomas grew irritated.

"I think…I think we left them in the chapel."

"Shit!" Thomas kicked the chair that was bolted to the floor; it flew across the room.

Danielle looked slightly disturbed by his power and anger. "Okay, come on," she placed her hand on Thomas's back, "We'll get out of here."

Thomas shook his head, "We need…to…go…" He trailed off as he spotted something on the wall, directly behind the doctor and Robin.

"What is it?"

Thomas merely motioned to the wall behind her.

Danielle spun around, "Holy shit," she muttered.

Behind the two carcasses, on the punctured wall carved in blood was a large number '1' and directly beneath it, 'Finish It' was scribbled, once again in blood. They both grew closer to the two bodies, only to notice the gruesome scene that fell before them. Streaks of blood lead from Robin's body to the wall, her limbs torn from her torso. Her arms thrown against the wall; her legs cut cleanly from her lower body. Her head was crushed beneath the carcass while blood dripped from the trunk of the neck.

They both turned from the mess. "I can't believe…" Thomas held his stomach, "Let's just go."

"What does that mean?" Danielle pierced her lips, "One…"

Thomas was already through the threshold, "It only takes one to finish it? Who the hell knows, this mother fucker doesn't make any freaking sense!"

Danielle scampered out the door behind Thomas, "The chapel isn't far. It's right over –"

"I remember where it is," Thomas stepped back into the shadows, followed by Danielle.

The chapel stood silent in the strobe lights, just awaiting more victims to join the psychopath doctor who once roamed the halls of that very cursed asylum. He was burned underneath the chapel in passageways which have been sealed off for years.

"Finally," Thomas grunted. "That seemed a lot further than last time."

Danielle situated her hand on the door, "We've come this far, let's grab those tapes then book."

"Wait, wait, wait," Thomas grabbed her arm. "We got to keep in the shadows and avoid anything that will attract that bastard back to us."

Danielle glanced over to him, "What do you propose?"

"Fuck it," he murmured after thinking for a moment, "we don't have much of a choice." He placed his hand on hers, together they thrust open the door.

The sunrise showed through the busted stained-glass windows, creating an eerie essence to a heavenly sanctuary. They didn't need to walk far, the tapes and cameras lay in the center aisle, right next to the very last pew.

Thomas rushed over to the pew and bent low, "Finally, here." He grabbed up the two cameras and stash of tapes.

"Okay, good," Danielle shuddered. She twirled back to the door, "Let's —"

The doors slammed shut in her face. A loud twisting, rumbling whine reverberated throughout the chapel.

"Shit!" Danielle tugged on the doors. "It's locked!"

Thomas dropped the evidence and dashed over to the entrance, "No, no, no! How'd this happen?"

"He set us up..." Danielle trailed off.

"Now how the hell are we going to...?" Thomas thought for a moment. "Wait, wait, didn't Max come in here looking for some hidden exit. Like a trap door or something?"

A smirk developed across Danielle's face, "You're right. You're absolutely right, but where would it be?"

"Not a clue, we'll just have to pan out and search for it." Thomas circled the room, "You know we'll have to go get Scott before we get out of here for good, right?"

Danielle glared at him, "I don't know if I can come back in…again."

Thomas shook his head, "We have to get him, there's no way I'm going to leave him behind."

"You're right, you're right," Danielle cried out. "Let's find a way out first and then work on the details."

They searched for another door to lead out; the only door noticeable was the entrance that was now sealed shut. The podium still sat crashed on top of one of Robin's fake, but lifelike mannequins. Thomas inched his way around the podium and finally came upon a squared away trap door on floor after he caught his foot on a small opening which seemed to be the handle to the door.

"Hey, Danny," Thomas bellowed. "I think I found it!" He bent down on one knee and grabbed hold of the fissure in the floor. Thomas heaved with all his strength. It gave after only seconds.

Danielle dashed over, a handful of tapes in one arm and the two cameras in the other. "Here, give me a hand with this."

He reached out and grabbed one of the cameras off her hands. She handed him the tapes as well, "Wait, wait; let me stash these in my pack."

The tapes slipped out of her hands; they fell down into the dark tunnel below. "What the hell are you doing?"

"You're not getting this," she stared at him with malevolence.

Thomas was taken back, "What are you talking about?"

"I know what the figure means."

"What? You're really freaking me out here, Danny," Thomas trembled.

"He wants us to finish our movie, he's turning our investigation into a horror movie," she clarified.

"What's the one supposed to mean?"

"That only one of us can survive!"

Thomas's face grew pale, "How do you know that?"

"Think about it," she began. "In any horror movie, how many people survive?"

Thomas thought for an instant, "Um, it's been years since I've even seen a horror movie. I don't really like them."

"One, it's always supposed to be one," Danielle bellowed. "One killer, one survivor, that's how they're supposed to work!"

Thomas stepped backward, "How the hell do you know that? "How do you know that thing is a he? And how do you actually know that…that monster wants to make a horror movie. Maybe he just wants us to finish exercising the building, or maybe to just leave."

"No!" Danielle outburst, she pulled the camera back, and let it swing. It slammed into the side of Thomas's skull. He crashed to the ground, his eyes shut, but still slightly twitched. "I planned this shit, you son of a bitch!"

He could only groan as he rolled around in pain on the cold, damp concrete. Blood poured from the side of his head; shards of plastic slammed to the ground around his body. Thomas tried to pull himself up, only to hurtle back to the ground. "No, please…" he muttered ever so silently.

Danielle pulled out a syringe from her jacket, "Here, stay still. This will only take a second." She brought the needle down to Thomas's neck.

The warm, paralyzing liquid overwhelmed the throbbing pain from the insertion of the long needle of the syringe. Once more, his eyesight blurred, and he grew dizzy. Even before he passed out, Danielle began to drag him from the chapel.

"Careful now," Danielle mockingly suggested, "We don't want you to smack your head." Danielle grinned wide, her cackle echoed through the entire asylum, sending chills down her own spine.

His hands sifted slowly along the brick wall behind him. A cold, steel plate protruded from the wall. Thomas grabbed hold of a bar which rested in the center of the plate that was about two foot by two-foot perimeter. He shuffled his feet to the right; another bar was attached to the center of a square. Thomas stepped to the side once more, another square, another bar.

"The morgue..." Thomas muttered. He swung around toward the wall of graves; Thomas fell to the floor; still woozy from whatever he was injected with.

Thomas glanced up to the entrance to the morgue, which led from the laboratory. Michael's gutted body flashed in his head. Puddles of blood gathered below the table, Michael's stomach had been stitched up after the figure pulled his insides out.

It enjoyed killing, the figure and the doctor had been a tandem, he thought. *The doctor filmed while the figure was killed. They worked together, why was he killed? The doctor must have been Danielle. She attacked me. She had to be.*

Bright lights flashed on in place of the flickering ones. Danielle stepped out of the dark corridor; she dropped a small box with three buttons on it, a red, a yellow, and a green. "Man, I've wanted to shut that shit off from the very start."

"There's no more to tape," Thomas whispered.

"What did you just say?" Danielle demanded; a smile still pierced across her lips.

"You don't need the doctor because you don't need anything to be filmed."

Danielle grew closer, "Wait, you think I needed the doctor?"

Thomas shuddered, "How could you do this? Our friends, your fiancé..."

"You think I cared?" she cackled shrilly. "Do you think any of them mattered?"

"You're sick! You're fucking insane!" Thomas's head still dizzy, he leapt toward her but collapsed.

Danielle grabbed his collar, "Get up before you embarrass us both." She slammed him back against the wall.

He faltered slightly as he tried to stand, then fell back against the wall, "You're a fucking monster!"

"Well, the killer is a monster, but I don't think anyone specified what kind."

Thomas's eyes grew wide, face twisted, "What?" The two paused momentarily. The smirk still amassed upon her mouth, "There's another isn't there?"

Silence filled the room; Danielle stepped backward, once again toward the secret exit.

"The doctor wasn't enough to restrain some of these guys and you couldn't have done this all on your own," Thomas assumed.

"Ding, ding, ding," Danielle mocked. "You are correct sir." She bowed and motioned to the entrance, much like a butler.

A voice boomed from behind her in that corridor, "Do you understand now?"

"Finish it…" Thomas murmured under his breath, "Finish it…Finish the movie. Son of a bitch," he lowered his head.

"You are a smart one aren't you," the voice echoed. The figure finally entered the light, the dirty white mask and skull painted bandana hid the true identity of the mastermind behind the massacre.

Thomas held himself up on the bars behind him, "You know, you mother fuckers…"

"What?" Danielle got in his face, "Please, please, tell us."

Her smirk irritated Thomas, "I began to think there were actual apparitions." He paused as the figure stepped toward him, directly beside Danielle. Its knife glimmered in the bright light. "But no, you're just two sick, sadistic, pieces of shit! Why did you do this? Why?"

Danielle grabbed a handful of Thomas's dark black hair, "You really want to know why?"

The figure pulled her off of him, "Come now, you're no better than them if you act like them."

Danielle turned her back to Thomas, and then spun around swiftly, "The money!" She slapped his face, "It's all about the fucking money!"

"No!" the figure opposed. It shoved Danielle aside. "It's all about the ratings."

Thomas began to escape from his drugged daze, "But you…"

The figure pulled the mask over its head and untied the bandana simultaneously, "The ratings, Tom."

"Alex!?" Thomas shouted, very confused. "What? Why?"

Alex tossed the mask toward Thomas, "Well, she's right too." Alex pulled Danielle toward him. He pulled her lips toward his as the two met. Alex shoved her back, "Ratings lead to money, of course."

Thomas, still stunned, attempted to turn away from the two murderers, "How could you do this Danny?"

"No!" Danielle dashed toward him. The knife she grabbed out of Alex's hand smashed against the same cheek which was broken open earlier.

Thomas fell to the ground, his cheek bled once more. His hand draped over the bloody wound, "Fuck you!" He spat a mouthful of blood toward Danielle and Alex.

"Well Danielle," Alex pulled her back toward him, "I think it's about time to end all this."

Danielle grinned, "We've got a few more hours of fun, wouldn't you say?"

Alex thought momentarily, "They'll start demolition in about three hours or so."

"Why are you doing this?" Thomas stepped forward from the wall. "You would have made the money anyway! You two are just as psychotic as Stroyne, murdering innocent –"

The butt end of the skull encrusted knife swiftly shattered Thomas's orbital bone; blood sprayed against the wall and dripped down the side of his face, directly over the open wound on his cheek. Thomas fell back against the wall and then fell to the concrete floor in sheer terror.

"The media my friend," Alex boomed. "You remember what happened with that one Batman movie, right?" He waited for a response from Thomas but only received a crushed look. "Ledger died and the film exploded into this huge blockbuster. So did anything else associated with him come to think of it. Paul Walker too. Those Fast and Furious movies shot up when he died! Shit, we can tack on Carrie Fisher to that list too. Not that Star Wars ever needed it, but you know…" He trailed off. "Can you imagine what will happen when the reporters and media assholes show up? They'll find the entire crew dead, the star of the movie with the knife in his hand, about to kill the producer who came after getting a call from the co-star for help."

Thomas's eyes grew wide. "I didn't kill…" he trailed off. "You son of a bitch!" he tried to gain his footing but fell once more after Alex plunged the knife into his thigh and ripped it open. Blood spilled out onto the floor; it trickled down his leg and built up a puddle on the floor where he lay.

"Never curse in front of a woman!" Alex demanded.

Thomas grumbled in pain, "Yeah, quite the woman you got there."

Alex apparently took offense to his remark and charged toward Thomas, the knife rose above his head, "I'll teach you some fucking manners!"

Danielle stepped in his way and grabbed the knife ever so gently out of his hand, "Now hold up a second Alex."

He gave her a confused look, "What is it? We should finish this now!"

"Let's get that brain dead cameraman first," she snickered.

Thomas stood and darted toward Danielle, all in one motion. He was stopped in his footsteps as Alex swung his blade around toward Thomas. Thomas's left hand suddenly went completely numb; all three people heard four distinct thumps on the floor. Thomas glanced down to his hand, his face grew pale. All four fingers, excluding his thumb, now lay on the floor, blood squirted out rapidly. "Oh shit," he fell to the floor once again, in even more pain. He blacked out immediately as he hit the floor.

"Look through my bag," Alex pointed toward the corner of the room to a black satchel. "We need to close up his wounds," he insisted. "We can't have a dead serial killer. Especially since we have to have our climactic battle before it's all said and done."

Danielle smirked as she turned for the bag, "What am I looking for?"

"Just look in there," he grinned. "You can't miss it."

After a moment of exploring Alex's sack, Danielle grabbed hold of a plastic handle and wrenched it upward. "An iron?" The metal, triangular tool was rusted throughout and seemed to be in too bad of shape to actually work.

Alex chuckled as he pulled up Thomas's arm. "Any other suggestions?"

"No, no, this works," Danielle agreed. "But were you planning for this?"

"Well," Alex sneered, "when in a position of mine, you must be prepared for the worst."

She laughed loudly, "But seriously, how did you know to bring this?"

"Think about it." Alex paused and propped Thomas up. "You were all here experiencing crazy shit. You can't tell me you didn't think someone would get hurt," he winked to Danielle.

She handed over the iron, "Here, does it need a charge or something?"

"Battery operated, come on Danny. You know me better than that." Alex flipped the red switch on the iron to the 'on' position. "This shouldn't take long. Go get Scott"

Alex turned the iron on and placed the flat, scorching side of the iron on the stubs which used to be his fingers. Thomas twisted and writhed in pain as he grabbed hold of his fingerless left hand.

Upon Danielle's return with Scott, Alex set the tripod up in the corner of the morgue and pointed it towards the center of the room. It overlooked Michael's mutilated body, covered in dried blood from his cynic wounds. Thomas sat next to the metal table where Michael lay. Thomas's face was enveloped in the very skull mask and bandana that Alex wore during the murders.

Thomas began to stir; Danielle quickly bent down and grabbed his left hand.

"Shush now," Alex squeezed his now burnt-closed, fingerless hand tight. "This is nothing compared to what your friends went through."

"Fuck you," Thomas muttered from behind the skull painted bandana. Again, he grabbed for his left hand. "What do you want from me? You've got everything you want."

Alex glared at him, and then suddenly grinned. He pointed to Danielle, "Fight her!"

"Whoa," Danielle raised her arms as if to surrender. "I thought you were going to fight him in some climactic shit?"

Alex hugged her forcefully, "I am…" He gazed into her eyes, "Right after he kills you!" He pulled out a switch blade and stabbed her in the back, right behind her kidneys. "I *am* sorry, but only one can survive."

Danielle stepped backward, grabbed her side as the pain stretched from her back all the way around to her stomach, "How could you? I loved you." She went flying into Thomas as Alex shoved her violently to the floor.

Luckily, Thomas caught her before her head smashed off the concrete. "You bastard!" Thomas bellowed.

"Finish her!" Alex shouted.

"Fuck you!" Thomas stood as he helped Danielle back to her feet, blood still poured from her back. Thomas was draped in a flood of her blood.

Alex slowly wandered over to the two, "She's going to die anyway, that wound is fatal. Just put her out of her misery."

"No!" Thomas shuddered. "Hell no! I will not drop to your level, you…you coward!"

Alex strolled toward the tripod; he clutched the camera. He moved the play button to pause then sauntered back to Thomas and seized his fingerless left hand.

"Get away from me!" Thomas yelled and pulled back from his grasp.

Alex slammed the knife deep into Danielle's abdomen as she crashed back to the floor toppling Thomas in the process. She screamed in excruciating pain.

"Here," Thomas held out his left hand to Alex. "Do what you wish! Just please stop torturing her!"

Alex reached in his satchel and pulled out a roll of clear duct tape. He placed the knife in Thomas's palm and wrapped the tape around the knife and his hand. "There, that wasn't too painful was it?"

Thomas sat in silence and held Danielle's head in his lap, "What do you want me to do now? Kill her after you tortured her?"

Alex plunged his knife deep into Danielle's throat, puncturing her main arteries and shooting blood all over the black cloak which Thomas now dawned. "No, I'll kill her, you just need to look like the killer," Alex snickered and turned back to the camera.

"No! You bastard!" Thomas bellowed.

Danielle coughed and curled; blood poured from the gash in her neck as well as her mouth. It discharged onto the floor, seeping all over Thomas, and leached toward Alex and the tripod.

"Shut the fuck up!" Alex rushed back towards Thomas. He smacked him viciously with the base of the knife. "You're going to ruin this!"

Thomas toppled over beside Danielle and then glanced back at Alex.

He threw off Thomas's mask and grabbed his jaw vigorously, "Look into my eyes!"

Thomas stared into Alex's gaze, a glare of pure evil, "What the fuck do you want now?" He looked back toward Danielle.

"Oh, her?" Alex smiled, "She was just a pawn. After I had her shot up in the lab, the doc and I threatened Danielle in the seclusion room. We told her that we would torture her more than we already had unless she helped us. So, she didn't exactly have a choice, you see?" An evil snicker appeared across his lips, "We stuck an earpiece in her ear and directed her. She is - well was a good actress."

Thomas grimaced in pain, shock, and disbelief. "No!" he shook his head then turned away. "No!"

"Look at me." Alex paused and waited for Thomas to make eye contact once again. After he glanced toward him again, Alex continued. "If you speak and do not listen to what I say, I will kill him," Alex said quite gravely and pointed toward Scott.

Thomas's eyes opened wide; he nodded with no other choice available but to go along with Alex's insane plan in order to save Scott's life. Danielle's was already past saving.

 Alex pulled the mask back down over Thomas's face then rushed back to the camera and clicked on the record button. He grinned behind the tripod; his plan finally seemed to come together.

Thomas hovered over Danielle; on the camera it seemed as though he had just slain her. He shook his head in disbelief, "No…" he whimpered quietly.

Scott had been pulled up from his fetal position in the corner of the room across from the tripod by Alex. Alex held the switchblade to Scott's throat, Danielle's blood still dripped from the knife. "Drop the knife and take your mask off you son of a bitch!"

Under the mask, Thomas looked shocked. He thought to himself, *What the hell is he doing?*

'Do it or he will die,' Alex mouthed behind the camera as he tightened the knife around Scott's neck. Blood began to trickle down his neck where Alex held the knife.

Thomas shook his head; he tried to shake the taped knife away from his hand. On the camera, it seemed as though he was waving the knife toward Alex, who smiled wide once again. Finally, the knife fell loose and plummeted to the concrete floor.

"Show me who you are!" Alex barked.

Slowly, Thomas reached across his face with his right arm. He wrapped his fingers around the mask and loosened the bandana then pulled both over his head, revealing his identity.

Alex shook Scott manically; ready to deal a fatal blow. He then clicked off the camera, the red light vanished. The knife had been drawn closer and tighter to Scott's collar.

"Don't do it!" Thomas shouted; the mask and bandana still grasped tightly in his hand.

"I have no choice!" The knife was driven through Scott's back up to his collarbone. It surfaced through his neck, blood sprayed across the room. As Alex withdrew the blade, Scott slammed to the floor. He spasmed briefly but then coughed up a mass of blood that combined with the blood that already secreted from the knife wound to create a large puddle at Alex's feet.

Thomas rushed forward, "Scott!" He fell to his knees and reached for Scott.

"Get back there!" Alex kicked Thomas backward. He flew back onto Danielle. He clicked the camera back onto record, "Okay Thomas, it's over. I'm calling the cops!" He reached for the emergency phone beneath the tripod.

"You won't get away with this, you sick son of a bitch!" Thomas called out from the floor.

"With what?" Alex smirked, "Surviving your onslaught of all of your friends? You're a fucking monster!"

Thomas's face twisted, "No, you can't do this!"

"You slaughtered them all! Cut them open and mutilate their bodies," Alex taunted him. "How could you?"

Thomas glanced down toward Danielle, then over to Scott, "Why?"

"What'd you say?"

"I said why! Why are you doing this?" Thomas demanded.

Alex seemed to grow irritated, "I already told you, you murderer! I want this to be over with!"

Thomas found his footing and made his way up to his feet, with help of the table where Michael's mutilated body still lay.

"I'll fu…call the cops!" Alex bellowed, as he almost forgot his role. He sauntered back to the tripod to switch the camera off once more.

Right before he could reach the camera, Thomas charged at Alex and knocked the switchblade from his grasp. Thomas leaped on top of him, tried to subdue him, but to no avail. Thomas grew weaker by the minute, his loss of blood finally caught up with him. His face grew pale, arms grew frail, and his legs could no longer support his weight.

Alex snatched up the switchblade from the floor and jammed it deep into Thomas's already bloody thigh.

Thomas writhed in pain, rolled around the floor. He grabbed hold of the small switch blade and wrenched it from his leg. Thomas covered the wound with his right hand.

The knife fell to the ground as Alex now charged at Thomas. Quickly, Thomas snatched the knife off the ground, rolled over, and shoved the switchblade in Alex's shoulder. He crawled up against the wall, the knife still wedged deep in his muscle.

While Alex rested up against the wall, Thomas rushed to his feet and fell to the opposite side of the room. Thomas grabbed the skull encrusted knife from the floor which had been taped to his hand. He then faltered over to the tripod and grabbed the emergency phone that lay where Alex dropped it. He swiftly dialed '911.'

"Yes? How can we help you?" the voice on the other side of the phone rang out.

Thomas shuttered and stumbled around with his words, "We need help! The crew...they're all dead! Please!"

"Calm down sir, where are you? Who are you? Who gave you this number?"

"Alex... Kinkaid...he did this! We're at the asylum!"

Alex bellowed from his resting spot along the wall, "What? Are you going to blame me for this? You monster! You killer!"

Thomas tried to block out Alex's voice and turned his back to him.

The voice paused, "Elizabeth Anne Asylum?"

"Yes, exactly!"

"We'll send out the local police immediately!"

Hope finally filled Thomas, "Thank you very much –" he fell to the floor.

"Fuck you!" Alex smacked him with the tripod, the camera crashed to the floor beside Thomas.

Thomas's vision began to blur then quickly shook it off. He kicked Alex's knee as he fell to the floor in a heap. "Don't fucking move!" Thomas pointed to Alex with the skull knife.

Thinking Thomas would not kill him; Alex stood and pushed himself away from the wall, the switch blade knife still wedged in his shoulder. "We aren't so different, you and I."

"How so? You're a killer and…I'm not."

Alex knew the camera was still on the record setting, so he continued with his act, "You have that backward my friend. But we both want money, fame, and the truth to be known."

"No, you want to kill you fucking liar!" Thomas shouted abruptly.

Alex stepped forward once more, "I think this asylum has fucked with your head," Alex motioned to his head. "I think you're switching our roles Tommy."

"No! No! No!" Thomas again barked, waving the knife in Alex's direction. "You're a monster!"

"Oh, is that why *you're* trying to kill *me*?" Alex asked gruffly. "Is that why you killed your own crew? Because you think we're all monsters?"

Thomas stepped back, "I didn't do this! I don't know why you keep acting like I committed your evil!"

"I can get you help, Tom. The best in the business," Alex tried to persuade him. "Just please, put down the knife."

Once again, Thomas grew angry. His face twisted and contorted; Thomas swung the knife near Alex. He sliced Alex's neck, very slightly, but enough to force him to fall back and slam his head against the wall.

Without hesitation, Alex grabbed out the switchblade from his shoulder and pounced from the wall simultaneously. He swung wildly at Thomas, slicing his leg wide open, right above the knee.

Thomas collapsed, dropped the knife, and clutched his open wound with his hands, "Fuck!" he shrieked in pain. "Why are you doing this? You win already. You've got your movie; the crew is dead so it's all yours! Just leave, no one will know you were here!"

"What are you talking about? This is your plan, you crazy son of a bitch." Alex flashed a smirk toward Thomas.

"You're the damned psycho!"

Alex turned his back toward Thomas, "There *is* a fine line between genius and insanity."

Thomas tried to stand, but the cut above his knee prevented him. "Ahh!" he bellowed as he collapsed once more.

"Trying to escape?"

Thomas inched back toward the wall, "What are you waiting for? Are you going to kill me?"

"Why would I kill you?" Alex scratched his head with the sharp edge of the knife. "I would stoop to your level if I did that."

"I never killed anyone!" Thomas demanded, "Never!"

Alex cackled softly, "Well maybe inflicting some pain will remind you, the same way you tortured all of your victims."

"Fuck yo –" Thomas was instantly taken back by sudden shock. Blood poured down the side of his face; he reached up to stop the hemorrhage, his ear was missing! In a spat of rage, Alex sliced his ear clean off.

"More pain so you can feel what your victims - our friends felt," Alex roared.

Thomas rolled in pain, his hand draped over the side of his head where his ear was once attached, his other hand over the wide gash above his knee, "I can't feel…I…I…"

Alex, knowing both men were out of camera view, charged Thomas, he threw his leg forward directly into his temple, Thomas's head bounced off the concrete floor but had lost consciousness before his head hit the floor. Alex threw himself on top of Thomas, "You have no idea what I can do to you," he whispered into Thomas's still attached ear. He then crawled on his hands and knees over to the camera, still on its side and slid the record button into the off position.

Derrick Smith

Chapter 13

FREE AT LAST

"You got point," four police officers wearing Kevlar vests and bulletproof helmets stood at the asylum entrance. Each equipped with a submachine gun. The lieutenant took the lead. "Dan! Wake up!" he roared.

The officer to his right snapped to attention, "Sorry sir!" he apologized to the lieutenant and kicked open the door.

One by one, they filed in. "You guys see anything up there?" The last officer shined his flashlight into the rooms which lined the still bright hallway.

"No, but I have a bad feeling about this Chris," the lieutenant murmured to the last officer in line.

The four ventured through the treacherous rooms and secret passages, no casualties occurred for their small group. They passed the only modernized wing in the building, updated for the crew.

"Careful now," the lieutenant announced, after he motioned to streaks of blood spread along the floor near the chapel entrance.

"The call came from the northeastern corner of the building," Dan, the officer on point proclaimed.

The group headed into the chapel, traveled slowly, cautiously. The lights inside grew much dimmer than those in the hallway. All four policemen trekked to the altar where Robin's dummy still lay crunched under the podium. They quickly realized it was a fake and began to question the legitimacy of the supposed motive of the investigation.

"Wasn't this supposed to be some sort of paranormal investigation?" Dan questioned.

The lieutenant nodded his head, "Yes, it was supposed to be."

"Why is there a doll crushed under a podium? Tyler, weren't you some sort of specialist with this crazy shit?" Chris inquired.

"Yeah, well I don't know what the hell they were planning," Tyler informed the group. "But this company, Atomic Skyz, has never really been the best source for reality. They always seem to extend the truth, and well…"

"From the looks of it, they extended it alright," the lieutenant finished.

"Okay, so if the call didn't come through here, there must be some room behind this place where it came from," Dan suggested.

The lieutenant turned back to their entrance, "Well let's look around for –" He stepped on a crinkled up, thick packet of papers. "What's this?" he grabbed the packet.

"It's the floor plans…" Chris pointed to a scratched-out spot on the map, "Look here…"

The four law enforcement officers gathered round, "I'm guessing that's where it came from, but –" Dan was cut off.

"There's no entrance though," the lieutenant pointed out.

"It must be some secret room this fucked up doctor added in," Tyler suggested, "I've heard about it in newspaper articles a few years ago."

The lieutenant turned his light away from the map, "Okay, let's head that way then."

"It's through the morgue, right?" Chris questioned.

"Yeah," Dan agreed, "it's right next door."

The autopsy room door burst open with the force of four men, those four men were the policemen in charge of rescuing whoever was left in that hell hole. The lights were just as bright as the hallway, and the room reeked of death.

"Freeze! Everyone, put...your..." Dan trailed off.

"Where are they?" the lieutenant demanded.

Chris and Tyler circled the perimeter, right before they discovered the secret entrance to the morgue, screams echoed throughout the autopsy room. The four police froze and backed together slowly. They circled the room, searching in every corner for where the screams derived.

"There's got to be another room in here," Tyler insisted. "We aren't deep enough to be in the Northeastern point."

The lieutenant broke apart from their small formation, "He's right, we need to search for..."

"Here!" Chris cried out, "There's light from behind this…this…table, I guess."

Tyler rushed over to the supposed entrance and reached low for a grasp on the metal table which seemed to be pulled in front of an open doorway. "Come on Dan, give us a hand!"

It took three policemen to shove the table out of the way, "How many people do you think it took to prop this up here?" Chris asked the group.

"Man, I have no clue," Dan uttered. "I mean, it took almost all of us just to push it out of the way."

"Okay guys, come on now. Be ready," the lieutenant reminded them of their situation.

The three other men recreated their previous formation. Dan once again took the point position, and the lieutenant was the first to step into the gloomy abyss. Light shined through the small passageway from the opening at the end of the tunnel.

Alex held Thomas on top of him with all his might, unconscious from the extreme blood loss. "Where the hell are they?" he murmured to his comatose foe.

After nearly five minutes of supporting Thomas's weight so awkwardly, Alex began to shout out and acted as if he were in pain as he anticipated the reinforcements Thomas called for.

Suddenly, four large cops, draped in plenty of protection from head to toe, burst into the morgue. They all seemed to be in pure shock; "Freeze!" one officer warned them.

One man lay in a puddle of blood on the floor, a woman set up against the tombs on the other side of the room, blood soaked from her abdomen, and two men entangled in a tussle on the cold, concrete floor.

"Freeze!" the lieutenant barked. The others gathered behind him, all seemingly in shock.

The man on top of the pile was missing the fingers on his left hand, a knife wielded in his right. Blood poured from his missing ear onto the man below who also had open gashes stretching across his bruised and battered body.

"Freeze!" he repeated.

The men continued to brawl on the floor, "We will open fire!" Dan cried out from behind the lieutenant.

Gunshots rang throughout the morgue from all four policemen's firearms: smoke enveloping the room in a thick mist. Screams of pain overwhelmed the law enforcement officers, as they backed out slowly until the smoke cleared from their view.

Alex held Thomas close to his body; the knife held in his right hand was pulled close to his head. Another warning boomed throughout the room, "Freeze!"

"We will open fire!" another voice echoed.

Alex smirked very slightly; he glanced over to the tripod, once again recording from the corner of the room. He pushed Thomas upward, pretending to fight him back. He closed his eyes as he knew what came next. The gun shots blared all around him and forced Thomas backward off of Alex as he flew from his grasp like a rag doll. The knife dislodged from his grip as he rolled to the ground, blood sprayed from his wounds from the gunshots.

After the smoke cleared, the four officers inched their way back into the decomposing smell of dried blood. The lieutenant was the first to step forward, gun placed in its holster and rushed over to Thomas and Alex. "Are you alright?" he reached down for Alex who just rolled over.

"Thank God you're here!" Alex grabbed hold of the lieutenant and his point man. "He's insane, he killed everyone, all of the crew, everyone!" Alex heaved himself back to his feet with the help of some of the officers.

"We need immediate backup at the Elizabeth Anne Asylum," the lieutenant howled into his walkie-talkie on his shoulder. "There are multiple casualties, one survivor; the producer, Alex Kinkaid."

"Sir," Dan interrupted.

"What is it?"

"He's still alive," he stood from checking Thomas's vitals.

"Correction, there are two alive. The presumed murderer, Thomas Flynn, after being shot twice and cut multiple times, is still alive. We need medical assistance now!"

Alex faltered; he had trouble standing. "I have evidence showing it *was* Thomas." He grabbed hold of the lieutenant's arm for balance.

"Sit, sit, please," Dan grabbed his other arm, "You need rest."

Alex slowly sat down, next to the officers, "We were filming a movie, and I have it all on tape!"

"Please, relax," the lieutenant insisted, "we can worry about that later."

"Can I please make copies of those tapes?" Alex pleaded.

The cops glanced at one another, "Well, I –" the lieutenant began.

"I just don't want all of these guys – my friends, to have died in vain," Alex beseeched, nearly in tears.

"I suppose that will be fine," the lieutenant finally addressed, "Just make sure we get the originals ASAP."

Dan and Tyler flipped Thomas on his back, pulled his arms together, and bound them tight with zip ties.

"You're fine now," Chris proclaimed. "He'll be stuck in a mental institution for quite some time."

The lieutenant scoffed, "A little ironic, don't you think?"

"Lost his mind in an asylum and will spend his life in one," Alex joined in with the policeman's laughter.

The two officers viciously carted Thomas, still seemingly unconscious, out of the morgue, through the brick walled passageway back into the autopsy room, not paying any attention to Thomas's well-being. His head slammed off the solid walls, his rag doll body flailed over the tipped-over table.

"Come on, let's get you to a hospital," the lieutenant convinced Alex. Chris followed behind the two, out into the hallway where Dan and Tyler waited to cart Thomas off to the patrol car.

Alex scooped up the bag of tapes from the autopsy room discreetly as he fell in line behind the policemen's lead. "Hold up guys," he uttered as he faked a limp.

"No problem," Chris grabbed his arm for support.

"Thanks man," Alex stumbled forward.

The five conscious men ventured through the blood-soaked hallways to the entrance of the asylum, door busted in from the policemen's entry.

"Finally," Alex blew a sigh of relief, "Out of that hell hole alive!"

Dan and Tyler tossed Thomas's limp body into the back of one of the two cop cars and slammed the door. He awoke suddenly from the loud 'bang.'

Thomas lifted his left arm and slammed repeatedly on the bullet proof glass; shots of blood sprayed from his fingerless hand. "No!"

The two cops jumped back.

Thomas screamed, "You got the wrong guy!" He thrashed about inside the cop car, "Please! Listen to me!"

Alex shook his head as all of the cops stared in disbelief, "He still thinks I did this. He's nuts, man!"

The lieutenant opened the passenger door to the opposite car, "Here you go Mr. Tremblay."

Alex stepped forward, "Thank you sir." He turned to the rest of the group, "And thank all of you for rescuing me, I don't think anyone would have been able to stop that psychopath if you didn't come."

"Well we got your call," Dan affirmed, slightly confused.

"Yes, you said you needed immediate backup," the lieutenant confirmed.

Thomas snickered back in his confinement as Alex hobbled over to the open door, "He called," and pointed over to Thomas. "Remember, he tried to set me up."

Dan and Tyler walked toward the lieutenant's car and away from Thomas. "Who do we believe?" Dan whispered to Tyler.

Tyler simply shrugged his shoulders, "Not my call."

The pair hurried toward the lieutenant who had backed away from the vehicle. "Who do we believe?" Dan repeated to the lieutenant.

The lieutenant turned to Dan and Tyler, "Alex!" he stated loudly.

Both Dan and Tyler ducked quickly as though he had dropped a grenade, "Shh," Dan murmured.

"What? Afraid I'm going to hear?" Alex stood beside the car.

The lieutenant stepped forward, nudged both young officers slightly. "After all," he began, "we are on his payroll."

Alex smiled wide from across the car; both officers stumbled back with Chris laughing quietly. "I own this mother fucking town!" Alex barked.

Back in the cop car, Thomas's eyes grew wide, "Son of a bitch!"

"Well?" Alex seemingly waited for the lieutenant to act.

"Well, what?" Tyler glanced quickly from the lieutenant to Alex back to the lieutenant.

The lieutenant raised his pistol from its holster, "Sorry, but you asked one too many questions," he smiled and glanced toward Alex.

He nodded his head in approval.

Two gunshots rang out; two bodies hit the gravel driveway, each with a single bullet hole in their head.

"Let's go," the lieutenant demanded, "This place gives me the willies."

Alex limped toward the back of the car, "Hold up, do you see something wrong here?"

Chris shouted from the steps to the asylum, "The prisoner is in the cab with no weapon and there are two officers down…shit!"

"Thank you Captain Obvious," Alex shouted back, "Get rid of them."

The lieutenant bent down and grabbed hold of Tyler's legs, "You going to help me?" he asked Chris.

"You better," Alex warned Chris. "We need to get back and report this *now!*"

Chris tossed his newly lit cigarette on the ground and stomped it out, "No prob."

The two policemen dragged the two corpses around the side of the asylum; Alex followed them with a shovel he grabbed out of one of the trunks. They all left Thomas alone in the cop car; the only thing for him to do was to imagine how many other crooked cops were on Alex's payroll.

"The station doesn't actually know you're here, do they?" Alex questioned as he began to dig a shallow grave.

The lieutenant looked back over his shoulder, "They know *I'm here*, but as for the others…no one knows where they are."

"Good, same old then?" Alex sneered and tossed the shovel aside.

The two officers rolled the bodies into the barely two foot deep grave.

Chris rubbed his hands together, "There, another job well done."

"You think you're done?" Alex snickered; he pointed to the shovel. "Bury them."

He shook his head, "Son of a bitch. I always get the bitch work."

The lieutenant stood back and laughed, "Yeah that used to be my job."

"Now you get promoted and get the easy work, right?" Alex smirked.

Chris piled dirt over the two deceased bodies, "Now we just report them as missing." He grinned back toward the two others.

"Let's hit it," the lieutenant declared.

Alex chuckled, "And make sure that bastard is still locked up."

The window Thomas had beaten on was bloody and cracked, he apparently tried to escape.

"Wow," Alex seemed surprised, "I thought those things were bullet proof."

Chris ambled over to the window, "It is, but I guess it's not —"

Thomas punched through the glass, shattering it to bits. He grabbed Chris's head and pulled it in through the window.

"Please, no!" Chris mumbled.

"Come on now Thomas," Alex pleaded with him. "There's no way you're getting out of here. Let's make a deal."

"Fuck all of you!" Thomas shoved on his forehead, a shard of glass shot through Chris's neck, cutting through his throat. He gargled something through the blood discharging through his mouth before falling to the ground in a lifeless heap.

Thomas jumped from the car through the broken window, "You mother fuckers aren't going to blame this shit on me!" He backed around the car, "Where's that damn phone?"

"You know that the ambulances and backup are on their way, don't you?" Alex asked. "You will be killed if you try to run."

Thomas continued to back away from the building, "I'll take my chances."

"If you stop and just back down, you'll still be a big star," Alex tried to convince him. "You'll be given the best treatment in jail you know. Anything you want."

The investigator turned away from Alex, ready to make a break for it, hobbling on one leg, still dripping blood from his hand, ear, and everywhere in between.

Thomas suddenly dropped to the ground as the lieutenant tackled him violently. He pounded on his back, "Don't try it!"

The lieutenant was shoved off just as quickly as he had taken Thomas down.

Thomas had kicked him backward; his head hit off the cop car. The lieutenant had fallen motionless next to the car.

Alex rushed to his side with the phone, "Here, here." He handed it over, "Just relax."

Thomas snatched it out of his hand, "You're done. This is over now!" He began to dial for help. "It's dead you bastard!"

Alex shrugged his shoulders, "I know." He pulled the lieutenant up, "You broke it."

"We'll just wait for the backup to get here," Thomas yanked the pistol out of the lieutenant's holster. "Don't fucking move!"

The lieutenant awoke after a few moments, "What the fu…"

"We're waiting for help," Alex assured him.

Thomas stood with the help of the pistol and glanced passed the gated entrance, "They should be –"

Alex kicked his knee out and Thomas fell back to the ground, "There's no one coming you prick!"

The lieutenant grabbed the pistol out of the gravel, "Don't move!"

Thomas tried once more to kick and squirm away; Alex pulled the pistol out of the lieutenant's hand, and smashed the butt end against Thomas's skull. "There," Alex declared, "We can finally get out of here!"

Thomas's body was dragged to the opposite cop car, bruised and battered and still bleeding badly.

Alex and the lieutenant locked Thomas's unconscious body in the back. "We need him alive, remember. He is the killer."

"Do we have proof?" the lieutenant questioned.

Alex held up the small bag of camcorder tapes, "All right here." He laid his head back on the seat and took a deep breath, "Shit."

"What is it?"

"The mask, I need the mask."

"Where is it?"

Alex glanced back toward the asylum, "Where do you think?"

"Fuck," the lieutenant grew irritated, "You going to get it?"

"I don't have a choice," he opened the door. "I'll be back, give me about fifteen minutes."

The lieutenant quivered, "Hurry up, I don't feel comfortable around this bastard."

"Shit," Alex screamed. He searched through the chapel, the basement, the autopsy room; everywhere. "Where the hell is it?" he barked.

Alex hustled back out the door less entryway. "Rick!" he shouted for the lieutenant in the car. "Rick let's just get the hell out of here! I can't find —" he jumped back.

The lieutenant's face was enveloped by the skull mask and bandana. Blood trickled down from the eye sockets. The cage separating the passenger and driver seat and the prisoner cab had been smashed in, Thomas was gone!

"Shit, shit, shit," Alex rushed to the car, wrenched the passenger door. "Rick, Rick, wake up!" he smacked his face repeatedly. Alex ripped the mask off his face, blood poured out from behind the mask. Rick's face had been beaten in; the cage must have torn through his flesh creating divots and deep lacerations equally spaced along his face. "Fuck!" Alex yelled at the top of his lungs.

Rick suddenly gasped, "He...he...took..."

"Quiet," Alex grabbed the walkie-talkie off of the lieutenant's shoulder. "Hello? Hello? Is anyone there? We need help! There's a murderer on the loose!"

The voice on the other end responded swiftly, "Where are you lieutenant?"

"This is Alex Kinkaid; the lieutenant has been attacked by Thomas Flynn, a crazed psychopath who murdered his entire crew of paranormal investigators. We are currently parked outside of the Elizabeth Anne Asylum."

"We'll be there immediately," the voice promptly answered, "Is the lieutenant still alive?"

"Yes," Alex explained, "He still has a pulse, but he is bleeding profusely."

"An ambulance is en-route," the voice clarified. "Keep pressure on the wounds with any sort of rag or t-shirt you have available."

"What about Thomas?"

"We'll find him, don't worry. Just try to stay calm," the voice assured him. "The troopers and ambulance should be there shortly."

Alex smiled, "I hope you catch him, that man is un –" he fell back onto the horn, it blared deafeningly.

The phone lay smashed in the passenger seat; Thomas used it to knock Alex unconscious. "Fuck you!" He reached for the keys, teetered over; the blood loss was kicking in once more. Thomas toppled back, out of

258

the car onto the gravel below. Once more, he blacked out, unable to escape the reaches of Alex and his corrupt lieutenant.

"Help, please!" Thomas yelped. His speech, however, was jumbled and unrecognizable. "Please, Alex is going to kill me!"

"I don't understand a word you're saying' my man," a large, husky man who wore a dark blue police uniform. "Let me take that thing out of your mouth, hold on," he reached around and pulled the choker from his mouth. "Okay, quiet now. I could get in trouble for this; you're supposed to be kept completely restrained."

"Thank you, thank you," Thomas muttered. "Alex is going to kill me! He killed everyone, he'll come for me!"

"Wow, you've been out of it for a while haven't you?" the man stammered.

Thomas tilted his head softly to the side; he tried to wipe the sweat from his forehead but could not budge his arms. They were tied behind his back, in a green jumpsuit. He was completely restrained, "Wait, where am I? What is this place?" Thomas panicked and began to shift side to side. He quickly realized he was bound to some sort of metal cart. His legs and arms were tied while he was standing.

The man chuckled slightly to himself, "You've been in and out of comas for a good nine months." He walked over to Thomas, "We're on our way to your trial."

"Trial? Trial for what?"

"Murder. Alex submitted a video of the killings, and you were shown as the killer behind that skull mask of yours," the officer unlocked the wheels under the cart. He began to push him forward.

"It wasn't me! It was Alex!" Thomas shook his head rapidly, "No! How did he set me up? How?"

"I saw the tapes, and uh…I'm sorry I don't think he set you up."

"What do you mean? I didn't do this!" Thomas wobbled the cart. "It was Alex! Alex!"

The man in the uniform pushed him forward, through the doorway where they sat. "Oh wait," they stopped abruptly. "Better put this back in."

"Wait, no, please! It wasn't me, ple –" the choker was shoved back into his mouth.

"Sorry about that my man," he pulled up Thomas's sleeve. His arm was covered with small red dots. "I'm sorry about this too."

"Nnnnn!" Thomas tried to scream; tears built up in his eyes. He shook and quivered.

The man shoved a long needle into his arm, "This will hurt quite a bit, but uh…I'm sure you're used to it by now."

Thomas twitched and trembled, "Nnnnn!" he shouted once more. His pupils grew dark, nearly black, his head quaked sadistically. His head finally fell motionless, eyes closed once more.

"There, back in a coma," the uniformed man again pushed him along the hallway. "Bailiff, can you please open the door?"

The door at the end of the hallway opened slowly, "Thank you sir." Thomas's comatose body thrust through the open wooden entryway.

"All rise!" the bailiff commanded. "The judge presiding over today's hearing will be the honorable Judge Smith."

"Nearly thirteen months ago, the brutal Elizabeth Anne Asylum Massacre occurred," explained the female reporter. "Nine innocent people were mercilessly slaughtered; possibly more as two police officers were reported missing that same day. Of those nine, one policeman was slain most viciously. Eight others were members of a ten-man paranormal investigative team. Only three people survived, "Thomas Flynn, Alex Kinkaid, and his brother, Lieutenant Richard Kinkaid. Thomas was a paranormal investigator and the lead investigator in their examination of the Elizabeth Anne Asylum. Alex was, and still is, the executive producer and owner of Atomic Skyz, the new reality television network that showcases actual events with no special effects or actors. He voluntarily oversaw the company's first major motion picture shot at that very asylum, which was just introduced into theaters a little over a week ago. The lieutenant was called via emergency phone by Alex after he was assaulted by Thomas earlier in the day and also was brutally battered by Thomas."

The reporter continued, "After being in and out of comas for approximately nine months after the horrific slaughter, Thomas was tried and convicted of first-degree murder. The verdict was attained just moments ago, greatly due to the amount of footage collected from the videotapes filmed during the production of the Atomic Skyz movie, named *Reel Fear*. Thomas's motive apparently was due to his anger towards Alex's company going so commercial, after they resorted to utilizing fake haunts and haunted house props, and losing control of his show, which he originally created with one of the victims. His plan was seemingly to make all the deaths look like poltergeist attacks by wearing a skull mask and bandana," she held up a replica of both, "much like the one I have here. He went insane and began mutilating one crew member, making the murder seem as though it was an old, inhumane, asylum remedy used by Doctor Stroyne, the owner and head medical expert of the time. Thomas apparently had an actor play a doctor type character and helped him film and murder those numerous innocent paranormal investigators. That actor was also executed by Thomas's hand later in the night."

"The tapes were taken directly from the cameras used inside the asylum," the reporter held up a replica video tape, "and it appeared as though Thomas was going to compile the sadistic murders to create an 'all too real' reality movie. He was sentenced to life in the newly re-established Elizabeth Anne Asylum due to schizophrenia and a borderline, unspecified personality disorder. During the times he was free from the coma, Thomas blamed the producer, Alex Kinkaid as well as his brother, Rick, the only police officer to survive who was called to rescue Alex. The video tapes easily disproved his theories and false accusations. The copies actually were given to Alex for the creation of the movie which was how all of the crew members lost their lives producing." The reporter paused, tears built up in the corners of her eye, she continued a she wiped them away tactlessly, "That is they very way he was given custody of them originally, by explaining that so many innocent people lost their lives creating that very footage and that if the judge did not give him the ability to finish their motion picture, then all of their lives would have been lost in vain."

"As you can see," the reporter smirked as she stepped backward, directly in front of a movie theater which had just left a screening of *Reel Fear*, "this travesty made into a reality movie, has hit the public big time. It has risen to the top of the charts, bringing in the most money in the first week since The Dark Knight back in 2008 with over $158,411,000 in the first weekend alone. Let's see if we can get someone's opinion," she said for a young adult, maybe mid 20's, "excuse me sir, ma'am."

The couple turned toward the camera, "Yeah, what's up?" the man asked.

"Would you mind giving us your opinion of the movie you just watched?"

"It was..." the woman stammered, "gruesome, sadistic, I can't believe they allowed them to put out real footage from a real murder."

Her partner cut in, "I thought it was amazing. It was just awesome how well all the angles were shot after being filmed using a camcorder; at least that's what I heard they used to shoot it."

"I'm just glad that sick, psychotic mass murderer was caught," the female chimed in.

The reporter grinned, "He was actually just prosecuted today, and he'll be spending the rest of his life right where he ended everyone else's."

"In a crazy bin?" the young man cackled, "That's ironic, don't you think?" He wrapped his arm around his girl and pulled her tight.

"Yeah, sure," she reluctantly agreed. "I heard that just a week ago, when this was released, was the exact anniversary of the massacre. Is that true?" she questioned the reporter.

The reporter nodded, "Yeah, that's true. I don't know whose idea it was to plan that, but it seems like it was quite a good idea," she turned her focus back to the cameraman. "I mean, look at the records, it's phenomenal how well this movie is doing. It's decimating previous ratings, it's raking in more money than any other movie, and it has helped *Atomic Skyz* become one of the most popular channels on cable –"

The television clicked off, "Damn, this thing worked out perfectly." He cackled over his over-sized mahogany desk. Alex guided his fingers through his thin, dark black and gray hair and blew out a thick puff of smoke from his cigar.

"No shit, this was the best one yet," Rick held his stomach while laughing. "You couldn't have planned that scenario better."

"Excuse me," a voice echoed over the intercom, "Mr. Kinkaid?"

Alex held his finger up toward Rick, "Yes, Susan?"

"Ms. Jackson is on line one."

Rick whispered to him, "I got to be going anyway."

"Thank you, Sue," he nodded. "I'll see you later. Put some of that shit on your scars that the doctor gave you, it might help," Alex recommended.

"Yeah, yeah, yeah," Rick joked as he grabbed hold of the door.

"Hey Darla!" Alex declared excitedly, "I told you, didn't I?"

Silence.

"I doubled our income. I got us the best ratings ever." Alex's facial expression dropped from excitement to disappointment. He set his lit cigar down in the ashtray on the corner of his luxurious new desk.

"So you did," Darla agreed surreptitiously.

"So…" he paused, "Do I get my raise?"

A slight cowl could be heard through the phone, "Can you repeat your success?"

"Excuse me?" he grew impatient. "Darla, I did the impossible. I made this small-time television company into one of the biggest, most popular production companies in the world."

Silence from Darla's end.

"How can you ask me to repeat this? That will be damn near –"

"Possible…it better be possible," Darla warned.

Alex swallowed hard, "You promised me the money Darla."

"If you do this for me, and make us *the* best, then we'll talk. Other words, you may end up like some of those poor souls that made our movie," she cautioned.

His cheeks flushed, eyes wide, but Alex was able to subside his feelings of fury, "Thank you, Darla." He slammed the phone down, "Fuck you!" He threw the phone from his desk, the cord pulled from the wall.

"Mr. Kinkaid?" Sue's voice once again shot through the intercom.

"What?" Alex asked shrilly.

Susan continued after a brief pause, "Is this a bad time, sir?"

"Is it ever a good time when Darla calls?" Alex sighed.

"Good point," Susan smiled through the phone.

Alex coughed as his cigar smoked away in his ashtray, "Um anyway, did you have something for me?"

"Oh, yes. Your one o'clock is here. Would you like me to reschedule?"

Alex thought hard, "No, no, that's alright. Send them in."

"Right away, sir."

"Oh Sue…"

"Yes sir?"

"Call that paranormal team, tell them to be ready to pop in bright and early tomorrow," Alex insisted.

"Not a problem, I'll get them on the line right away," she said. "Anything else?"

Alex paused, "Oh yes. Find that *Haunted Pennsylvania* book; we need to find a new and better location."

Susan's pen scribbled along the paper, "Anything for you, Mr. Kinkaid. Anything more before I send the two actors in?

"Not at all. Thank you Susan, now please if you would; send them in. We've got to get started right away."

"Yes sir, on their way in right now."

Derrick Smith

About the Author

Derrick Smith is an author, podcast host, paranormal investigator, and researcher with extensive experience investigating historically active and reportedly haunted locations. His work draws from field documentation, witness accounts, and historical research, blending factual methodology with narrative exploration.

Reel Fear marks his second publication with UNX Media and his first full-length feature outside of hist anthology series. Smith's debut collection, *All Monsters Are Human: An Unsettling Collection of Horror Stories*, was recognized as the Best Horror Author in Pittsburgh of 2025 by the Evergreen Awards.

Through his writing, Derrick examines how belief, expectation, and environment influence human perception, particularly when individuals attempt to manufacture or control the unexplained.

Derrick's podcast, The Other Side of the Bridge, is on the Unexplained Network: www.unxnetwork.com

Website: ironcityparanormal.org

Derrick Smith

Publications by Un-X Media

Haunted Independence Missouri by Margie Kay 2016
Gateway to the Dead: A Ghost Hunter's Field Guide by Margie Kay 2016
Family Secrets by Jean Walker 2017
The Kansas City UFO Flaps by Margie Kay 2017
Un-X News Magazine 2011-2026 in print and digital
A Sonoma County Phenomenon: Evidence for an Interdimensional Gateway
by Margie Kay 2019
The Fast Movers: Evidence for High-Speed UFOs/UAPs
by Margie Kay, Bill Spicer, and Larry Tyree 2020
Journey to Spirit by Devin Listrom 2020
Winged Aliens by Margie Kay 2021
The Remote-Viewing Workbook by Margie Kay 2019 (on LULU)
The Master Dowsers Chart Book by Margie Kay 2021 (on LULU)
A Sonoma County Phenomenon by Margie Kay 2020
Rules for Goddesses by Margie Kay 1999
The Alien Colonization of Earth's Waterways by Debbie Ziegelmeyer 2021
50th Anniversary of the SE Missouri Ozarks UFO Flap
by Debbie Ziegelmeyer and Margie Kay 2022
Meeting Wallace by Larry Costa 2023
Holiday Poems and Recipes by James Bair 2023 Cookbook
Dying to Meet Them by Mindy Tautfest 2026
Adult Coloring Books for meditation by M.K. 2023 -2005
Incident in Varginha: Space Creatures in the South of Minas by Vitório
Pacaccini and Fernanda Pires 2025
How To Research a Haunted House by Margie Kay and Violet Wisdom 2025
All Monsters are Human by Derrick Smith 2025 Fiction
Incident in Varginha by Vitorio Pacaccini 2025
UFO Attacks in Brazil by Thiago Luis Ticchetti 2025
We Got It From THEM! By Dr. Gregory Rogers 2025
Take a Haunted Roat Trip on Route 66 by Margie Kay 2025
IMPACT by Dr. Gregory Rogers 2025 Fiction
Reel Fear by Derrick Smith 2026 Fiction
Earth's Unseen Inhabitants by Larry Tyree, Bill Spicer and Lily Nova 2026

Documentary Films:
PORTALS; The Cube; Mysterious Missouri
And more!
Un-X Media is seeking authors who write books about unexplained phenomena,
alternative health, and esoteric knowledge. Contact us at www.unxmedia.com for
more information. Un-X Media and the Un-X Broadcasting Network are subsidiaries
of G&M Enterprises, LLC

www.ingramcontent.com/pod-product-compliance
Lightning Source LLC
Chambersburg PA
CBHW072346030726
47505CB00015B/2057